D0795451

"HEY! WATCH OUT!"

Dawn looked up and saw an object hurtling through the air toward her. It hit her squarely in the face, and she dropped to her knees, her head buzzing. Something warm trickled from her nose, and she tasted blood.

Two boys raced toward her from the field.

"Dawn! You all right?"

She tried to look up toward the boy who was talking, but the tears in her eyes and the pain filling her head made her look back down instead. She shook her head. "No," she half sobbed. "What hit me?"

"Soccer ball. I didn't see you or I'd have yelled sooner. I'm really sorry."

Dawn recognized the voice now. It was Nathan Hall. She'd been wanting to get to know him—but this wasn't the sort of meeting she'd had in mind. . . .

For adventure, excitement, and even romance . . .
Read these Quick Fox books:

Andrea's Best Shot by Dan Jorgensen

Crystal Books by Stephen and Janet Bly
1 Crystal's Perilous Ride
2 Crystal's Solid Gold Discovery
3 Crystal's Rodeo Debut
4 Crystal's Mill Town Mystery
5 Crystal's Blizzard Trek
6 Crystal's Grand Entry

Marcia Books by Norma Jean Lutz
1 Good-bye, Beedee
2 Once Over Lightly
3 Oklahoma Summer

DAWN'S DIAMOND DEFENSE

DAN JORGENSEN

Chariot Books
David C. Cook Publishing Co.

A Quick Fox Book

Published by Chariot Books,
an imprint of David C. Cook Publishing Co.

David C. Cook Publishing Co., Elgin, Illinois
David C. Cook Publishing Co., Weston, Ontario

DAWN'S DIAMOND DEFENSE
© 1988 by Dan Jorgensen

All rights reserved. Except for brief excerpts
for review purposes, no part of this book may be
reproduced or used in any form without written
permission from the publisher.

Cover design by Graphcom Corporation
Cover illustration by Jim Cummins
First printing, 1988
Printed in the United States of America
92 91   5 4 3 2

Library of Congress Cataloging-in-Publication Data

Jorgensen, Dan.
  Dawn's diamond defense.

  Summary: Dawn's ninth grade year is filled with her
work on the soccer team, her involvement in her church
youth project, and her determination to end a bitter
feud between two other girls on the team.
  [1. Soccer—Fiction.   2. Christian life—Fiction]
I. Title.
PZ7.J7688Daw   1988   [Fic]   87-11735
ISBN 1-55513-062-3

for Marie Highstreet
who would have been a great athlete
and who is a wonderful friend and grandmother!

Acknowledgements
Thanks to Holly Cybyske and Dave Eyestone
for their assistance, the Ray Anderson family for
the suggestion, and John Olson for his advice
and special encouragement.

Contents

1
Rough Introduction

"Hey! Watch out!"

The shout caught Dawn off guard as she rounded the corner of the gym near the high school practice field. She looked up from her book and saw an object hurtling through the air toward her.

Instinctively she dropped the book and pulled her hands up for protection, but it was too late. The object hit her squarely in the face, and she dropped to her knees, her head buzzing. Something warm trickled from her nose, and she tasted blood.

Two boys raced toward her from the field.

"Hey! It's Dawn! Dawn? You all right?"

Dawn tried to look up toward the boy who was talking, but the tears in her eyes and the pain filling her head made her look back down instead. She shook her head. "No," she half-sobbed. "What hit me?"

"Soccer ball. Gee, Dawn, I'm sorry. I was just working on volleys with Troy, and that one got away from me. I didn't see you or I would have yelled sooner. I'm really sorry."

Dawn recognized the voice now. It was Nathan Hall. He was a year ahead of her in school, and just this week she'd told her best friend, Carla, how she wished she could get to know him. This wasn't the sort of meeting she'd had in mind.

Several other guys, an older man, and a young woman came running up to join Nathan and Troy as Dawn moved from her knees and sat down, tilting her head back to stop her nosebleed. The woman slipped in between the boys and knelt down beside Dawn.

"Here, let me take a look at that," she said in a quiet voice. Gently she pushed Dawn's hand aside and whistled softly. "You're going to have a couple of black eyes and a fat lip out of this. What happened?"

Dawn's vision was clearing now, and she was embarrassed as she looked around at the boys. The man turned to look at them, too, and Dawn recognized him as the high school boys' soccer coach.

"That's what I want to know," he said sharply. "Who's responsible for this?"

"Sorry, Coach. I guess it's my fault," Nathan began. "I was working on my volleying. I didn't see Dawn until it was too late."

Dawn accepted a tissue from the young woman and then shook her head. "It's not his fault any more than it is mine," she said. "I came walking over the hill with my head buried in a book. I should've been paying attention to where I was going."

"Hey, gang! What's going on?"

Dawn was surprised to see Rev. Sobasky, the youth minister at her church, walking toward them.

"Oh, hi, Rev Steve," Nathan said with a little smile. "We just had a slight accident here. Kind of my fault, I think." He gave Dawn a sheepish grin, and she grimaced in return, thinking about what she must look like.

"Listen, I don't think we need twenty medics here to help this girl," the coach growled. "Everybody back on the field and start working on the passing and receiving

10

drills. Pair up and go hard for ten minutes." He paused. "Then we'll talk about how many wind sprints we'll be needing before we start the next drill."

The boys groaned and started back toward the field, but Nathan hung back.

"You going to be okay?"

Dawn nodded. "Yeah." Her nose had stopped bleeding, but now it was stuffed up and she couldn't talk clearly. "Don't worry."

"All right." He gave her a big smile, and she felt weaker than when she'd been down from the blow in the face. She'd told Carla Nathan was one of the cutest boys she knew. As he stood there smiling, the soccer ball in the crook of his arm, she was positive that he was.

"See you later." He loped off toward the field, stopping to drop-kick the ball back where Troy was waiting.

"Coach, you better get on back with the team," said Rev Steve. "I'll make sure Dawn is okay. If North Park's going to take the conference this year, they're going to need your guiding hand every minute."

"That's for sure," the coach answered, getting to his feet. "We're really young this year, but, who knows?" He shrugged. "Glad to see you out here again this year, Reverend. Let me know what you think after you get a chance to watch for a while."

He gave a little wave, smiled toward Dawn, and headed back to the practice field. Rev Steve knelt down in his place and touched Dawn's bruised face. Then he turned to the young woman, who still knelt close by.

"I'm Steve Sobasky, a minister at Dawn's church," he said, extending his hand. "The kids all call me Rev Steve."

"Nice to meet you," she replied. "I'm Susan LaFollette. I'm a senior at the college, but I was down here today working on my soccer kicks and checking on

11

the field. I'm assistant coach for the ninth grade girls this year."

"You are?" Dawn said, sitting up straighter. She pulled the tissue away from her nose so she could talk clearer. "I'm going to try out for the team, I think. We heard we were getting a new coach, but we didn't know there was a new assistant, too."

"Yup, that's me," she said with a grin, pushing back her curly brown hair. "Actually, there isn't an assistant coach position, but the school's letting me help because my boyfriend is your new coach. I play on the college team and I volunteered to help."

"Great," Rev Steve said. "This is kind of a rough way to get introduced, but meet one of your players, Dawn Davis."

Susan held out her hand to Dawn, and Dawn shook it self-consciously. Susan was small and slender, not much bigger than Dawn. And she was pretty. Dawn brushed half-heartedly at her tangled hair, realizing again how frightful she must look with a fat lip and a tear-streaked face.

Dawn was careful about her appearance. In fact, she'd thought about giving up soccer this year, because it sometimes got rough and she ended up with a lot of bruises. Her mother and father wanted her to quit, too, but now that she had met Susan, she suddenly committed herself to playing once again.

"Did I hear the coach imply that you're a regular out here?" Susan asked Rev Steve as they stood.

"I'm sort of the unofficial team advisor," he said with a chuckle. "The Polars are my adopted team." He looked out at the practice field. "I haven't played much since college—had a little semi-pro experience before going into seminary—but I enjoy watching—and giving advice!"

"I didn't know that," Dawn said. "I thought you

12

were just a minister." She hesitated. "I mean, uh, you know . . ."

Rev Steve laughed again. It was a big, booming laugh for such a mid-sized man. "I know. Listen, if you two don't mind, I want to go over and get a closer look —see how they handle some of the drills."

"Go ahead," Susan said. "I'll stay and talk with Dawn." She shook hands with the minister again before he turned and walked over to the practice field. Then she turned back to Dawn.

"I've got to go get my ball, but I'll be right back. Okay?"

Dawn nodded and leaned back on her hands, watching as Susan bounded gracefully over to the smaller practice area near the main field. Deftly she scooped up a soccer ball, almost without pausing, and hurried back, slightly out-of-breath.

"I like to come down here to work on my shots because that little goal is always in place." She pointed toward the net on the smaller field. "I was out there kicking the ball around when I saw you go down. Man, you fell like you'd been shot or something." She planted the ball firmly on the ground and sat back down on the grass.

"I did fall kind of hard," Dawn agreed. "Nothing like getting smashed in the face with a soccer ball to wake you up in a hurry."

"Or put you to sleep in a hurry," Susan said with a grin. "So, tell me, what position do you play?"

"Center fullback. Defense is kind of dull, but I like it."

"Oh, come on!" Susan chided. "There's no such thing as a dull position in soccer if you play it right. And, if you weren't there to play defense, it wouldn't matter how many goals your team scored, because the other team would get it right back. Right?"

"Yeah, but our eighth-grade coach was really big on the girls who played offense. Course, we do have a real good attacker—Wendy Marks. She's a striker and she really knows how to get the ball to the net. We won a lot of high-scoring games 'cause of her."

"What kind of scores?"

"Oh, 4-3, 5-4. Lots."

Susan laughed. "Real defensive battles, huh?"

Dawn noted the twinkle in Susan's eye and joined in the laugh.

"Sure. We made Wendy the hero lots of times, because she had to score one more goal for us to win." Dawn sobered slightly. "Are you a defender?"

"Well, no. Actually, I'm a forward." She wrinkled her nose at Dawn's frown. "I know, another one of the glory spots. But, believe me, I know how important those defensive positions are, and so does Alan."

"Who's Alan?"

"Alan Young. My boyfriend and your new coach. He played midfielder on his college team last year. He's never coached before, but I just know you're going to like him." She smiled. "I sure do."

Dawn laughed and then put a hand to her mouth. "Ow, that hurts. I suppose I look like Godzilla by now?"

Susan eyed her carefully. "Well, not exactly Godzilla . . ." She paused as if thinking of some other creature to name, then reached over and patted Dawn on the shoulder. "Don't worry. You're just a little swollen. You'll be fine in a couple days." She stared out toward the field.

"The boys' team looks a little rusty, especially on defense!"

They watched as Nathan dribbled the ball into the space at midfield and kicked a lead pass to his friend Troy. Troy dribbled the ball past his wing defender and touched a crossing pass to Kirk Woodard, the Polar's best returning player at the right forward position. Woodard controlled the ball, made a move on the defender, and chipped the ball back to Troy, who scored on a great shot past the center defender.

"That was a nice play," Susan said admiringly.

"Sure, for the offense," Dawn answered. "The defense looked a lot like ours."

"What did he do wrong?"

"I don't know. I guess he got suckered in by Troy." Dawn pointed to the spot where the shot had been made. "See, Troy set him up and used the center fullback as a shield. Then the goalie couldn't see what he was doing, and when Troy kicked past the defender, he got it past the goalie, too."

"Well, you certainly seem to know what the trouble is," Susan said.

"I can see what's going wrong; I just don't know how to correct my mistakes," Dawn answered. "Our coach last year never had any good advice, so we just struggled along and hoped Wendy would score more than the other team."

"Well, maybe Alan and I can do something about that," Susan replied. "How's your volleying?"

"Okay. I can kick hard and far, but I'm not very accurate. If that had been my volleying instead of Nathan, I probably would have hit the person walking by nine out of ten times."

"I'd say that's real accurate," Susan said with a smile.

Dawn laughed. "Yeah. Never thought of it that way." She stood up, feeling a little wobbly, and waited for her head to clear. "Guess I'll try to head home. See you at practice next week."

"Right. Monday at three."

Dawn had only covered a few yards when she was stopped by a shout from Susan. The college student kicked the ball in her direction; Dawn neatly stopped the ground ball with her toe and rested her foot on it.

"Let's see some of that kicking power you were talking about," Susan said. "Show me some distance, okay?"

"I don't know. My head hurts a little." Dawn shrugged and eyed the ball. "I'll give it a whack." She drew her right foot back and smacked the ball with her instep. It sailed a good thirty yards.

"Not bad," Susan said, "especially since you're wearing street shoes. You doing anything tomorrow at eleven?"

Dawn shook her head.

"How about coming up to the college and watching my team play? We're scrimmaging St. Pete's—a little pre-season warmup."

Dawn nodded. "Maybe. I'll have to see."

"Okay." Susan waved again. "If not, then I'll see you Monday, for sure."

She jogged back toward the practice area, retrieved her ball, and began kicking. Dawn watched for a few seconds and was about to leave for the second time when Nathan came running to catch up to her.

"Look, Dawn, I'm really sorry about hitting you," he said. His face was streaked with sweat and he had dirt on one cheek, but Dawn still thought he looked cute. Self-consciously she put her hand up by her swollen lip.

"It's okay. Really. I know you didn't mean to."

"Well, thanks. Both Troy and I are excited about getting invited to try out for the varsity. I've been concentrating so hard on my game that I haven't been paying much attention to things around. We're the only sophomores invited up, you know," he added proudly.

"That's great," she said, dropping her hand and smiling. "Well, maybe I'll see you later."

"Sure," he answered. "You going out for soccer?"

"Guess so. We start practice Monday at three."

"We'll be practicing then, too." He stopped as if trying to decide what to say next. "Hey, how about if we meet at White's afterward and have a Coke or something? I'll buy. It's the least I can do after bashing in your face."

"I'll probably look like a real gorilla by then," Dawn answered, grinning. "You sure you want to be seen with me?"

He smiled, almost shyly. "Yeah. I'm sure."

He was interrupted by the coach shouting his name, and his smile changed into a worried look. "I better get back or I'll be running laps until then. See ya Monday."

She waved as he hustled back to the field, then reached up and touched her swollen lip. For the past month, she'd been trying to make herself look pretty enough to attract Nathan's attention. Now a fat lip and a swollen nose had done the trick. *How weird could things get?* Dawn wondered as she soccer-kicked a pine cone out of her path and headed for home.

2
Double Trouble

"Dawn!"

Rev Steve was calling and walking rapidly in her direction.

At this rate, I'm never going to get home, Dawn thought as she watched the minister walking toward her. She like Rev Steve—all the kids did—but she'd been avoiding him lately. She wasn't sure she wanted to keep going to Sunday school this year, and she didn't want to talk about it. Fewer of her friends were going, and none of the teachers was very interesting.

"Hi," Rev Steve panted as he reached her side. "Didn't mean to desert you back there, but I wanted to see how those younger boys worked against the older ones. I think both Nathan and Troy have a real good shot at starting, even if they are just sophomores."

He was an average-looking man with reddish-brown hair that never seemed to stay in place. His heavy-framed glasses gave him the look of a professor, but his toothy grin reminded Dawn of a picture she had seen of Huckleberry Finn. She had seen Rev Steve jogging from time to time, but up till now she hadn't known about his involvement with soccer.

18

"Anyway, how you feeling?" he continued.

"Okay. A little sore. My lip feels worse, but my nose feels a little better."

The minister laughed. "You're going to have a couple of doozies of black eyes by morning, I'll bet." He sobered quickly as Dawn's face fell. "Sorry, I know that's not so funny to a fourteen-year-old. It happened to me when I was a freshman playing soccer. I just made out like I was some big sports hero. Suppose that would work for you?"

She shook her head, then brightened. "You really like to come out and watch, huh? Wish I'd known last year —maybe I could've got some advice when I was playing so lousy."

"What position?" he asked.

"Defense. Center fullback."

"No kidding!" He looked at her with surprise. "Why, I'm an old sweeperback myself!"

Now it was Dawn's turn to look surprised. "Did you play it all the time?"

"Nope. Like everyone else, I wanted to be the star. You know, scoring all the goals. But I had a good coach who convinced me that the defense was as important, if not more important, than the offense, and I stuck with it. There are no drums and bugles for a good defender, but there's a great feeling when you help win a game by stopping the other team."

They heard a shout from the boys' practice and turned back toward the field to see Troy punch the ball past the goalkeeper for a score.

"Looks like they're scrimmaging now. The coach has a pretty green team, so he asked me to come out and show them a few things about defense. Right now, they're just playing 'run up and down and score.' They need some work on holding their positions."

Dawn nodded. That was her biggest weakness, too.

She never knew when to challenge the ball and when to hold her ground.

"Well," Rev Steve said, wiping a hand across his brow. "I guess I'll go over and watch them work out a little longer. I won't start anything with them until Monday, but I wanted to get an idea of who was on the team. Glad you're feeling a little better."

He waved and turned away, then turned back. "See you in church Sunday? We're going to get the new Sunday school sessions going this week."

Dawn frowned. "Maybe. I mean, I'll be in church, but I don't think I'll go to Sunday school this year." She gave him a sheepish smile. "Maybe I'm getting a little old for that stuff."

"Maybe you just need a change of pace," he responded. "I'm thinking of a youth forum this year for the high school kids, and we might as well put the ninth graders in there, too. I might even lead it myself, if I can get the right person to lead the adult forum that I usually do."

"Well . . ." Dawn began.

"But," he said, holding up both hands, "don't let that stop you from coming, okay? I promise I'll let some of you have a chance to talk, too." He grinned. "Really. Give it a try. You can always quit, you know."

"Maybe I'll come. But just for the first session, to see what it's all about. Okay?"

"Deal," he replied, waving again and jogging off to the practice field.

"Good grief!" Dawn said aloud. "First soccer and now Sunday school. And I wasn't even going to walk this direction on the way home."

"Wow! Who won?" Carla asked, as Dawn opened the door to her friend on Saturday morning. Dawn had to admit that she looked like she'd been in a prize fight. Both eyes were black, her nose was still slightly swollen, and her upper lip was fat and tender.

"The ball won," she said. She pulled Carla inside and filled her in on the previous day's experience, including meeting the new assistant coach and Nathan's invitation for Monday.

"At least I got a date with Nathan out of it," she concluded. "Well, sort of a date."

"That's great!" Carla exclaimed. "But are you sure you want to go out in public?" She flipped on Dawn's radio and dropped into a beanbag chair.

Carla was Dawn's best friend and also the owner of the most beautiful eyes in North Park Junior High. On the best of days, Dawn's eyes were no match for Carla's, but today Dawn felt altogether grotesque alongside her friend.

"At least the accident unscrambled your brain and got you to come back out for soccer," Carla said, drumming her fingers in time with a song on the radio. Carla was a regular on the team, alternating between left and right center forward. "I knew we were going to have an offense, but I was beginning to wonder about the D."

"Come off it," Dawn replied, plopping down on her bed and crossing her legs. "I'm *on* the defense, but we won't win any games because of me. Any of the other girls could take my spot."

"I doubt it. Besides, I think you'll have it a lot better on defense than I have at midfield."

Dawn laughed. "Yeah, you have to keep peace between Wendy and Karin."

"Wendy Marks, World Scoring Champion," Carla said. "Too bad she doesn't have some personality to go along with her athletic ability."

"Do you think there's going to be trouble between her and Karin?"

"Of course." Carla pushed back her long, sandy-colored hair and settled deeper into the beanbag. She

21

had a pretty face and soft features, but was muscular with a stocky build. Wendy liked to call her "baby tank" when she played—a remark that hadn't endeared Wendy to any of the girls.

"One thing's for sure," Carla added. "Karin's going to give Wendy a run for her money. She really didn't get much of a chance to show us what she could do after transferring in so late last spring. But I've watched her working out on her own, and she's a good player. She's got a lot of scoring moves as good as Wendy's."

"I like Karin," Dawn said. "She goes to my church and she's always real nice. Pretty quiet and shy, though. I think it's hard for her to make friends. She was pretty upset when her folks moved here from Brownsville."

"She was a star player for them, too. I talked with a Brownsville girl at the fair a couple weeks ago, and she said Karin was their leading scorer last year—in spite of missing the last two games by transferring here."

"Well, it sure made Wendy mad when Karin scored a goal in the last game here against Valley."

"Did it ever!" Carla agreed, sitting up straighter. "You'd have thought the world was ending. Sometimes I just can't believe Wendy's for real."

"She gets a lot of pressure on her from her dad. Tricia said he's always pushing her to be the best."

"Oh, that's right," Carla interrupted. "I forgot to tell you. Tricia says Wendy's dad is setting up a scoring trophy for the junior high soccer league this year—one for the boys and one for the girls. Of course, you know who he's expecting to win for the girls!"

"You're kidding!"

"Seriously. He's going to have the league present it to the leading scorer. He owns the newpaper, you know, and his photographer will take pictures and everything."

Dawn shook her head in disbelief.

"Some people are just weird," Carla concluded. "Sometimes I wonder how Tricia can be Wendy's friend, anyway."

"Oh, Wendy can be okay," Dawn inserted. "And Tricia's awfully nice. Maybe she sees Wendy as her own personal project to influence for good. Besides, *somebody* has to be Wendy's friend."

Carla giggled and nodded her agreement. "I'm just glad it's Tricia and not me." She got up and walked over to the window. "Want to go out and kick the ball around for a while? Practice starts Monday, you know."

"Okay, as long as you don't kick too hard. I'm still a little stiff and sore. Maybe we can practice for a while and then bike over to the college. I told Susan that I'd come by and watch her team play. We might even get a look at our new coach."

"You think he's a fox, or what?" Carla asked as they started outside.

"Probably an 'or what,' with our luck. Besides, we'll all hate him, anyway, after the first couple times he makes us run wind sprints." They groaned together at the thought.

Dawn set up in her defensive position and spent the next fifteen minutes fielding Carla's half-speed kicks.

"Wow, am I out of shape!" she puffed after missing a kick and having to run it down. "Maybe this isn't such a good idea—I mean my going back out for soccer."

"At least come out and give it a try," Carla responded. "You can always quit."

"I've been hearing that a lot lately," Dawn muttered.

"What?"

"Oh, nothing. Just talking to myself again." Dawn picked up the soccer ball and twirled it on her fingers. "You're getting good at kicking this thing. You should really be able to set up our scorers with your passes."

23

"Sure, if they'll just get along with each other. Who knows, we could even be league champions this year." Carla gave a little laugh, grabbed the ball off Dawn's fingers, and drop-kicked it over the backyard fence into an open field. "Of course, we have to get someone out there to stop the other team once in a while, too. You guys play defense about like that fence."

She dodged out of Dawn's path and ran to retrieve the ball.

Dawn walked across the yard and sank down under a tree, wiping perspiration from her forehead. It was only ten-thirty, and already it felt like ninety degrees. On top of that, there was no breeze, and the leaves above her hung limply in the mid-morning sun. She exhaled loudly, groaned, and leaned back against the tree trunk, closing her eyes. She sat quietly for several minutes, wondering where Carla had gone, when her friend's voice shattered the silence.

"Hey, lazy bones! Wake up! We've got company."

She opened her eyes and blinked in surprise at Carla and Karin Gardner, their newest teammate and classmate.

"Hi, Karin." Dawn waved, but stayed leaning against the tree.

Karin gaped at Dawn's appearance. "Hi yourself," she responded. "Carla was just telling me about your accident, but you really look awful."

"Thanks."

"Oh! I mean . . . well . . . I'm sorry."

"Just kidding," Dawn said. "We were just talking about you. What're you doing over this way?"

"She was out running in that field," Carla volunteered, pointing toward where she had just kicked the ball. "Can you believe this girl! I think she's trying to show us up on the first day of practice." She laughed at Karin's embarrassed look. "I figured I'd better grab her before she got too good, and see if she wanted to go along to the game with us."

Dawn smiled and nodded. Karin looked almost too fragile to be a soccer player. She was tall and slender, and her long, strawberry blond hair flowed down over her shoulders, surrounding a slender neck. Her blue eyes had a worried look.

"I don't want to butt in on anything," Karin said softly. "You sure you want me to go along?"

"Positive," Dawn said emphatically, getting to her feet. "You got your bike along? We thought we'd ride over."

Karin nodded. "It's back there. I've been riding over every day to use the field. There's never anyone around, so it's a good place to run. I didn't know you lived here."

"I didn't know you were out there running, either," Dawn replied. "You trying to get ready for soccer?"

"Just the past week or so. I've been gone all summer to my grandparents' place in Massachusetts." She beamed. "I had a chance to go to a two-week soccer camp out there. Helped me a lot with my scoring techniques."

"That's what we were just talking about," Carla chimed in. "We figured we ought to have a pretty decent team this year with you and Wendy doing the scoring. All we need is Dawn's defense to shape up, and we could win the conference."

Karin's face darkened at the mention of Wendy's name.

"You think Wendy and I can play together okay?

"Why not?" Carla answered.

"I don't know. I guess I'm afraid Wendy won't want me taking any shots if she's got a chance first. I don't think she'll give me too many breaks, that's all."

"Well, maybe," Dawn said, "but she's just going to

25

have to learn to pass as well as shoot all the time. I doubt our new coach will let her hog the ball when there's someone as good as you on the team."

Karin looked at her feet. "Well, thanks. I'm glad you guys think I could help the team. But I'll just have to wait and see about Wendy. If we can't play together, I'll have to go somewhere else."

"Huh?" Carla and Dawn spoke together in surprise.

"My dad's been trying to get me into a private school near here. He thinks I need some extra ninth-grade computer classes in order to get ready for high school. I didn't want to go at first, but now I've been thinking it might be for the best. That way I won't have to fight with Wendy about soccer.

"I've got till the middle of next week to make up my mind, so I thought I'd go out for a couple of days of practice and see how it goes. I'd rather stay at North Park, since we live here, but I really love soccer. I don't want a whole year of hassles with Wendy—so the Academy might be better."

"Academy?" Dawn said quickly. "What academy?"

"Melrose Academy. It's not too far from here, I think. You know it?"

Dawn and Carla exchanged glances but said nothing. Karin looked from one to the other, waiting for a response. When neither spoke, she broke the awkward silence herself. "I'll go get my bike . . . if you still want me to go along?"

"Oh . . . sure," Dawn said. She watched Karin walk toward the field.

"I don't believe it!" Carla hissed between clenched teeth. "Didn't anybody tell her that Melrose Academy is North Park's arch rival?"

3
Special Help

It was a loud, noisy crowd gathered at the college soccer field, and the girls slipped self-consciously into a corner of the bleachers. After the blistering ride through the late-morning heat, Dawn felt wilted. She figured she made a dismal sight, with her banged-up face and perspiration dripping off her chin. To make matters worse, there was no shade for the seats lining the field.

The game already was well underway, and Dawn shaded her eyes to get a better look at the action of the field.

"There!" she half-yelled in excitement, pointing toward the far touchline. "The right winger with the long hair. The really quick one." Even as Dawn spoke, Susan justified the remark by taking a crossing pass and swiftly dribbling the ball into the open space at midfield, eluding a charging midfielder in the process. Just as quickly, she pulled to a halt and chipped a high, arching pass back to her left center forward, who was cutting between two defenders about thirty yards from the goal.

Both the goalie and the sweeperback shifted to challenge the girl as the ball sailed toward her, but instead of letting the ball land, the striker leaped high to meet Susan's pass and headed it back toward Susan.

Too late, the fullback and the goalie saw what was happening, but Susan was too quick and in great position. She took the return pass and slashed a hard, flat kick straight into the far corner of the goal.

The crowd erupted in loud cheers. Dawn yelled with the rest, and then motioned back toward the field as Susan set up at right forward.

"That was great!" she said. "The goalie didn't have a prayer."

"Yeah, but it was the passing and teamwork that made it work," Karin inserted. "That other girl might have scored, but her head pass back to Susan made sure the team scored even if she didn't. I'll bet Wendy wouldn't have passed it back!"

"Probably not," Carla agreed. " 'Course, she probably wouldn't have gotten a nice pass like that in the first place. Remember, that's *me* out there trying to make the passes."

The girls laughed, and Dawn relaxed a bit. It was the first time Carla had said anything to Karin since the talk about the Academy, and she could feel the tension lifting a little.

At halftime the score was still 1-0. Dawn got Susan's attention with her frantic waving as the college team came running off the field.

Susan broke away from the team and ran over to the girls.

"Hi," Dawn replied. "I got here."

"So I see," Susan said, panting. She wiped at her face with a towel. "Glad you did. Did you see my goal?"

Dawn nodded. "Great shot!"

Susan grinned. "Thanks. It was the pass from Tanya that made it go, you know? Nothing like teamwork, I always say."

Dawn glanced at Karin, who gave her a little smile in return.

"Oh, uh, Coach, I brought along a couple more members of the team, Carla and Karin. They're both front-line, like you."

Susan held out her hand to each of the girls and flashed a winning smile. "Great! I'm Susan, and you can call me that, too. I'm not quite up to being called Coach at this stage of the game. I'm just a kid yet myself!"

She took a close look at Dawn's face.

"Looks a little worse for wear yet, but you're up and around. How are you feeling?"

"Great, except for the heat. You must be about dead out there on the field."

"It's not the best," Susan said, mopping her forehead again with the towel. "But it's nice having such a big crowd to cheer us on. This is opening week for the freshmen—they were told they *had* to come." She laughed as she glanced around at the crowd. "Freshmen will believe anything."

"You mean they *didn't* have to come?" Carla asked.

"Of course not. But we're not going to tell *them* that. We figure if we've got to play in the hot sun, then the least they can do is sit here and cheer us on."

She looked over at Dawn. "Great defense, huh? Told you it was important." She looked toward the field where her teammates were gathered. "If you're still here at the end of the game, I'll introduce you to Alan. He's here with some guy from the town who helped him get the job at your school. Maybe you know him—he's got a daughter who plays soccer, too."

Dawn had a sinking feeling in the pit of her stomach. "Where are they?" she asked, almost afraid to look.

Susan pointed. "Alan's the guy with the blond hair and glasses. Kind of slender. He just stood up. Here—

let's see if I can get him to notice us."

She began waving wildly, and the young man grinned and waved back. Nice looking, but no movie star. Dawn looked away from her future coach and scanned the people sitting around him. She breathed a sigh of relief.

"Don't see anyone I know," she said, "but I don't know all the girls' dads, either, so—" Her voice caught as she saw an older man and a young girl walk up the aisle and stop beside Alan.

"You've got to be kidding!" It was Karin who spoke as she, too, spotted the pair standing next to Alan, laughing and joking with him. The coach swung around and pointed in their direction, and Susan waved again.

"That's them," she said. "You know them?"

"Sure do." Dawn tried to sound normal.

"Well," Susan said, "I better get back or they'll start the second half without me. Take care." She hurried off, and Dawn sank down on the bench.

"Doesn't that figure," Karin said, still staring in disbelief toward Alan. "Just when I think there's hope, the new coach shows up with the enemy."

Dawn glanced over at Carla, who looked just as miserable as Dawn felt. Across the bleachers they could still see Alan, Wendy, and Wendy's dad, smiling and talking together.

By Sunday, Dawn's face felt better and didn't look too bad, either, with the help of some carefully-applied makeup. But even so, Dawn insisted that her family sit in the back row at church. She left quickly when the service was over and headed for the youth room in the basement.

By the time Rev Steve showed up, it was apparent that few kids had turned out for this first meeting. But the minister smiled and signaled for the half dozen present to gather around for an opening prayer.

Then Rev Steve looked around. "Looks a little grim so far, huh?" He chuckled. "When the others hear how super this little gathering really is, I just know there'll be a rush to get involved."

The kids laughed nervously, withholding judgment.

"This is going to be a 'do-something' forum," Rev Steve continued. "It's time the kids in this church took a look at some of the problems in this world—and started taking action."

Dawn was interested, but before she could ask what he had in mind, another student spoke up.

"Like what, for example?"

"Like picking a place where people are going hungry, finding out everything we can about it, and then seeing if there's anything we could do to help. How about Cambodia? Thailand? India? Maybe Sri Lanka? Or some spots right here in the good old U.S.A.?" He was waving his arms as he talked, and now he stopped and stared hard at the small group.

"I didn't know there were places in the United States where people were starving," Dawn interjected.

"There certainly are," Rev Steve said.

"Like Appalachia?" asked Monica Lemery. She was the lone sophomore present.

"A good example," agreed the minister. "There are thousands of people in the mountain area of Kentucky and Tennessee who haven't enough food, solid roof over their heads, or warm clothing." He paused and wiped his brow. "Although that's not a problem this time of the year!" He regained a sober look. "But it's no laughing matter to those folks when the weather drops into the teens and it's rain mixed with snow and not a decent meal on the table. If there's a table to put a decent meal on in the first place."

"But what can we do? We're just a bunch of kids." It was Monica again, and her spoken words echoed Dawn's thoughts.

"That's what this forum is for," Rev Steve said. "You want to help people, but it isn't always easy to make things better. The government gets in the way, or the people themselves are too proud to accept your help. I want you to get down and figure it out for yourselves. Maybe, you'll find you *can* make a difference."

The hour flew by as the kids discussed project ideas.

"That was great," Dawn said to Rev Steve, as the kids headed for the door.

"Glad to hear you say that," he responded. "Now if you'll just recruit me some more kids so we can have a more representative group for our church. There are at least fifty high school kids in this congregation—and we get *eight* for our youth forum. Talk about lethargic."

"Talk about what?" Dawn said with a laugh.

"It means being in a deep sleep."

"Sort of unconscious, huh?"

They took a few more steps toward the door, and Dawn pulled up and turned toward him. "Remember you said you could show the boys' soccer team a few things about defense? Do you think you could show me instead?"

"Are you serious?"

Dawn nodded. "If you do, I'll try to get some more kids to come out for the forum. Promise."

Rev Steve chuckled. "Sounds like a bribe to me."

"I guess it is," Dawn answered, dead serious. "But why not? I need to improve my defense, and you need more kids. If you can teach soccer as well as you taught us today in the forum, I can't help but get better."

"Well," he said thoughtfully, "I could show you a few center fullback tricks. It's a deal."

They shook hands solemnly. "So when's our first

session?" asked Rev Steve.

"How about early tomorrow morning?" Dawn suggested. "We could meet over at the practice field near Hyde Park. It isn't used much, so nobody will see me making an idiot out of myself."

"You won't be." He grinned and put a hand on her shoulder. "But, Dawn, one lesson won't work wonders. If you really want to improve, we'll have to meet on a regular basis for a few weeks. That is—" he paused—"if you think it's worth it after tomorrow."

Dawn smiled. "Okay. What time tomorrow?"

"How about six?"

"Six a.m.! I haven't been up that early all summer." She groaned. "Wait'll you see me at six a.m. Talk about lethargic!"

"Don't worry," he responded. "You start seeing soccer balls flying at you out of the dark and you'll wake up in a hurry. Guaranteed."

Dawn walked home from church with her parents, her thoughts filled with the forum and the upcoming practice session. Suddenly she realized that her dad was speaking to her.

"Huh?" She shook her head and looked up at him. He was a slender, tall man with thinning hair and a warm smile.

"I said," he answered, "that you seem to be several miles away from here. That must've been *some* lesson in the youth forum today."

"It was," Dawn agree. "We talked about the world hunger problem."

"Maybe your generation will be the one to finally wipe out the problem of hunger in this nation—if not the world."

"That's what Rev Steve said. Our youth group is going to try to find a place where there's a real hunger problem and do something about it. We had a good discussion, and I said I'd try to get more kids interested. Everybody thought Sunday school was going to be boring this year, but it's not."

"Your mother and I had a good session today, too," Dad said, "but it's not as interesting without Steve up there. You kids are the lucky ones this year."

Mom laughed. "Maybe we should do what the kids are doing and study a current problem."

Dawn smiled. Not bad. Maybe the whole church would end up getting involved. She skipped ahead a couple of paces and kicked a stone out of their path. "Oh, and I forgot to tell you!" she exclaimed, turning around and walking backward. "Rev Steve said he'd work with me on my soccer defense. Did you know he used to play center fullback?"

"No, I didn't," Dad answered. "It's nice of him to offer to help you."

"We made a deal. He'll watch me, and I'll round up some more kids for the forum. Rev Steve was a little discouraged by the turnout." She hesitated. "Do you think it's okay? I mean taking on both projects—the forum and the soccer?"

Her parents both smiled.

"Yes," Mom answered. "I think it'll be just fine."

4
Breaking Point

"Now this," Rev Steve said, "is the 'flex' defense. It moves up and down with the flow of the play—almost like you're playing an accordian."

Dawn stifled a yawn and tried to focus on the small blackboard in the minister's hand. He had quickly drawn a few circles on the board, which was in the shape of a soccer field, and was pointing toward the defensive side. The early morning sunlight filtered through the trees, and birds sang cheerily.

"You've got to work closely with your goalie," Steve continued. "If you move one way or another, she's automatically going to compensate and cover the area where you're not. You two become a movable wall that nothing can penetrate. Does that make sense?"

"Uh, huh. I think so." She yawned again. "I'm sorry. Just a little sleepy."

"Well, let's get the blood flowing," he responded. "I'll bring the ball toward you, and you react to the shots. Then I'll have a better idea of what you need to do."

For the next twenty minutes, he peppered her with shots, bringing the ball straight at her and kicking it, then trying some sideways moves and sudden shots. A few times she made the stops, but usually the ball went flying past and into the net. Each time, she quickly pulled the ball out and booted it back to him, setting up for the next attack.

Finally, Steve pulled up, placed the ball firmly on the ground, and sat down.

"You're pretty good," Dawn gasped, flopping down beside him. The sun was rising over the trees now, and it was already getting warm. Another hot August day.

"Not bad for an old defensive player," he chuckled.

"How come you never played offense?"

"Because I liked defense. I always felt good when we shut down the other team and I was partly responsible. Usually the goalie gets most of the credit—but the first defensive unit has as much to do with it as anyone.

"Besides, if you play offense, you get criticized if you don't score. If you play defense, all you have to do is stop the other team. It's really a pretty simple game, right?"

Dawn laughed. "Right. So what are you going to do to improve my game? I looked pretty pathetic just now —especially trying to stop an *old* defensive player!"

Steve snorted and tapped the ball over to her.

"First, you've got to quit reacting so soon. Let your opponent commit to a move first, and then react. That way you'll either stop the shot or at least cause her to change plans. And, second, you've got to come out and challenge more. Don't just lie back waiting for something to happen. Get out there and challenge the ball and get it headed back upfield."

"Yeah, but I might really get bashed. Sometimes I'm afraid of being run down by the girl with the ball."

"Taking a hit is part of the game—" Steve held up a hand as Dawn started to interrupt "—sometimes it's going to hurt. But sometimes, you're going to save a goal."

Dawn swallowed hard and nodded.

"Let's practice stopping 'headers,' and then I'll show you how to dive at shots and knock them away with your head." He stopped and grinned as she wrinkled her nose. "*Then,* if you still think it's worth it, we'll set up a regular practice time for Saturday mornings. In a few weeks, you'll be an expert."

"Or one big scar," she giggled. "Then I can just scare all my opponents away."

By two-thirty, when the girls began gathering at the gym for the opening practice, Dawn was convinced that it was the hottest day of the year. She stepped into the gymnasium and had to support herself for a moment against the wall.

"You okay?" asked Carla.

"I think so. It's just the contrast between here and outside."

The girls took a few more steps into the gym and looked around. Several girls were sitting in a section of bleachers pulled out along the opposite side.

"Hey, Dawn! I thought you weren't gonna play this year." It was Beth Merriman, the team's goalie.

"I figured I better come back so you'll have someone to help you."

"Someone to blame, too, when they sneak those shots in," Beth laughed.

"Good thing you girls have me to even things out," a voice from two rows up interrupted.

"Wait, let me guess," Carla said sarcastically. "Who could that be?" She turned her back and waved off any comments. "Even things out, even things out," she mumbled. "Oh, I know. It must be someone who knows how to score goals so that our side can be in the game, too. Right?"

The other girls laughed nervously, glancing toward

Wendy, who was glaring at Carla.

"It's Karin, right?" Carla moved her hand from her eyes and turned around. "Oh, darn, wrong again. Oh, but what can you expect from a baby tank? Right?"

Everyone laughed harder—except Wendy, who sat back and folded her arms. "Go ahead and laugh," she said bitterly. "Without me, this team would be nothing but a loser, and you all know it—including you, Tank!" She spat the final words at Carla and tossed back her head.

Dawn shook her head. Carla probably deserved that, but neither of them would make things better with that kind of talk. It was too bad, though, that Wendy wouldn't treat the other team members with some respect. If she did, she'd probably be popular. She was kind of cute with her long, flowing blonde-brown hair, a thin but pretty face, and intense oval green eyes. She was taller than most of the other girls on the team and looked like she should be playing basketball instead of soccer.

But, snob or not, there was no question that the team relied on Wendy to do the scoring, and she was—at least at this point—their only hope for respectability in the upcoming season. Unless. . .

Dawn cut off her thought as Karin walked in, as if in response to what she was thinking. If Karin stayed and turned into the scorer Dawn and Carla thought she could be, they'd have an alternative to Wendy's bragging. Maybe that would bring Wendy down to earth. Suddenly, Dawn desperately wanted Karin to stay.

Several of the other girls greeted Karin warmly, and Dawn could see Wendy angrily eyeing her chief rival. Tricia Gillespie, the center forward who normally played on the same side as Wendy, and who also was Wendy's only *known* friend, was walking beside Karin.

"The new coaches are coming," Tricia said excitedly.

"They're . . . ," she stopped as if swallowing her next words as the two young coaches walked in behind her. Dawn joined the others in giggling at Tricia's reaction, then took a closer look at Alan. He was about six feet tall, had medium-length brown hair, and wore glasses. Susan was at his side, looking as bubbly as before. Alan seemed nervous.

The girls gathered around, and he asked them to sit down on the bleachers.

"I'm Alan Young," he began, stopping to cough, "and I'm nervous." The team members—now twenty strong —laughed, and he joined in. "I'm sure you've heard all sorts of rumors about me, but all you need to know is that I've been a soccer player for most of my life; this is my first coaching job; and I like to win."

He stopped and put a hand on Susan's shoulder. "This is Susan LaFollette, and she'll be my assistant. She's a senior at the college, and she's one good soccer player. And besides that," he added, "she's my girl friend, so watch how you act around me!"

The girls laughed, and Alan gave them a lopsided grin as Susan turned and gave him a little kick in the shin.

"Oh, yeah, that reminds me," he said, reaching down to rub his leg. "We've got some shin pads to hand out, and I want you to sign up for your uniforms. We'll hand out practice shorts and tops today and game uniforms next week. Now, how about everyone telling who she is, so we can start to learn your names."

Introductions went quickly as each girl told about the position she played and her soccer experience. Wendy proudly told how she had been the team's leading scorer for the past two years, and Dawn could see Alan smiling happily as she talked.

"She's got him wrapped around her little finger," Karin whispered. "I don't have much of a chance."

"Yes, you do," Dawn said, trying to sound more positive than she felt.

Following introductions, Susan talked briefly about some of the drills. Then Alan explained a new criss-crossing offense he hoped to have the team learn during the first couple of days. He and Susan went to the equipment room to pull out the practice gear and shin pads, and the girls seized their chance to talk.

"That offense looks a little confusing," Tricia said, leaning back against the bleacher seats with a sigh. "But I guess I'll learn it so I can save the rest of you and you'll be able to score."

"If it works like he just explained it," Carla replied, "even you and I will get a shot at the goal once in a while."

"It doesn't really work that way at all," Wendy said quickly. "I mean, my dad and I, well . . . we're sort of friends with the new coach, and he explained this offense to us already. Over at our house."

The other girls exchanged glances, but no one spoke.

"Anyway, he said that the wingers still do most of the scoring if the passing is done properly. Because you *do* want your best dribbler and shooter with the ball." She smiled confidently. "And, around here, that's the wingers. Besides, I'm out to win the new Metro League junior high scoring trophy. You all should want me to win, too, because it will be an honor for the team."

Before anyone could say anything, Alan shouted at them to come pick out shin pads and practice shirts and line up for game uniforms. Wendy jumped up and led the way.

"Around here, that's the wingers," mimicked Allison Braun, a reserve midfielder. "Blah on her." She stuck out her tongue in Wendy's direction, and the others around her laughed.

"This isn't a laughing matter," Dawn said quietly to

Carla, as they moved toward the pile of equipment. "I thought she was stuck up last year, but this is ridiculous. The whole team's gonna hate her before we even get on the field."

They took a couple more steps and stopped as Wendy suddenly grabbed a practice jersey from Karin's hand.

"That's mine!" she half shouted.

"Sorry, I didn't see your name on it," Karin replied cooly. "I thought we were supposed to go through these and pick out those that fit us."

"I always wear this number, and everyone knows it," Wendy snapped. "You knew it, too, so don't act so stupid."

Dawn could see Karin's face get red, and she pulled back the shirt as if she were going to whap Wendy with it. Instead, Karin forced a tight smile and gently laid it over Wendy's outstretched hand. "No problem," she said quietly, as the coaches emerged from the locker room and came toward the girls. "One shirt's as good as another as far as I'm concerned. Of course, I don't need special numbers in order to play well."

She gave Wendy a little shrug and turned her back before the other girl could answer. Dawn glanced at Carla out of the corner of her eye, and they both grinned.

The coach sent them to the locker room to get changed, and it was nearly four o'clock when they trudged slowly out the door into the blazing heat of the practice field.

"We're not going to do anything drastic today in this heat," he said, motioning them to sit down around him. "If the weather doesn't change for the better, we'll have to start practicing in the mornings, at least until school starts." He looked around at the girls. "Now, don't anyone take any chances out here. There's a water fountain on the side of the building, and I've got salt tablets if you need them. If you start feeling dizzy, get over into the shade and sit down."

Tricia raised her hand. "I'm feeling pretty dizzy already, Coach. Maybe I better just watch."

Carla snorted derisively as Tricia fell over in a feigned swoon. "You're always dizzy. How can you tell the difference now?"

The others laughed, and Tricia opened one eye and looked around. "No one ever believes me," she said. "I wonder why?"

"All right," Alan said. "I want some one-on-one passing drills from about twenty-five or thirty feet. Then we'll set up some cones and run a couple of group drills. After that, I want to set up the goalies on each net and have the rest of you show me what you can do with some one-on-one and two-on-one shots. Okay?"

Everyone nodded, and he clapped his hands. "Okay, then, let's fire up . . ." Alan glanced up at the scorching sun. "Bad choice of words?"

Several of the girls laughed, but most just groaned.

"Anyway, let's go." He clapped his hands loudly, and Susan quickly followed suit. All the girls clapped a few times and then broke into pairs. Dawn went with Carla, and Tricia singled out Karin.

Dawn saw the angry look Wendy gave Tricia's back. Then Wendy matched up with Amy Zobel, a reserve winger who sometimes substituted at Wendy's spot. She viciously kicked the ball in Amy's direction, and only Amy's quick reaction prevented the ball from hitting her in the stomach.

"And take it easy on each other!" Susan shouted, noticing the kick. "This is a warmup drill, not a 'kill your partner' drill!"

Dawn felt a little stiff after her tough morning workout, but after a few passes she began to loosen up. After about fifteen minutes, they formed two facing lines between two sets of cones, which Alan and Susan had placed about thirty-five feet from each other. The coach placed a soccer ball in front of the lead girl on Dawn's line.

"I want you to kick the ball to the front girl on the line facing you, then run along the outside of the cones and get in back of the other line," he said. "The girl who gets the ball has to quickly control it and then kick it back. Then, she runs around on the other side and gets in back of that line. Simple, right?"

He chuckled at their moan. "Just concentrate on making smooth, accurate, and quick passes. We should be able to get through the whole group in less than two minutes, and I'm going to time you. Ready—" he paused and raised his hand—"go!"

They raced through the routine and kept the ball reasonably within the boundaries. After they'd all gone through the routine once, Alan walked to the middle, frowning, "That took almost three minutes," he said. "You've got to work on speed and accuracy. Today, we'll blame it on the heat and the fact that you're just getting started. But by the end of the week if we aren't under two minutes, you'll be doing some extra running and LOTS of extra kicking." He stepped back. "All right, run through it again."

He put the stop watch on, frowned at the finish, but didn't say any more. After sending them for a drink of water, he had the girls form two lines again. This time he placed a ball in front of each line.

"Now, you've got four feet across here," he said, pointing to the distance between the cones. "Plenty of room to get two soccer balls to pass without hitting each other, right?" Several exclamations and laughs were the response. Alan grinned, too. "Dribble toward each other, then kick past each other to the next girl in line and get back in line yourself. Should be fun."

He signaled for them to begin and began chuckling as the girls battled to control the ball and make their passing kicks without interfering with each other. As they went through the line the second time, the drill began going faster and smoother, and Alan clapped approvingly.

Susan walked over with a clipboard, and they turned away to discuss another drill.

Karin came up on Dawn's line, and Wendy got the ball on hers. They started dribbling toward each other, each with considerable skill. As they prepared to make their passing shots, Dawn saw Wendy slide her left foot over and trip Karin. Karin stumbled forward, scraping her knee along the ground as her ball skidded ahead of her. Wendy completed her kick and with a smirk started toward the line.

Karin reached out and grabbed the ball, whirled, and threw it at Wendy, hitting her in the middle of the back. Wendy screamed and turned around, picking up the ball and starting back toward Karin, who was getting to her feet. Both coaches jumped between the girls.

"What's going on?" Alan shouted.

"She hit me in the back with the ball." Wendy said, a tear welling up in her eye. "She's crazy or something."

Alan looked angrily at Karin. "That true? You hit her on purpose?"

Karin nodded. "She knocked me down in the middle."

"That was an accident," Wendy said adamantly. "My foot slipped when I was getting ready to make my shot. Anyone could see that."

"I don't know what happened here for sure," the coach said, "but nobody on my team throws a ball at anyone else—EVER!" He turned to Karin. "That'll cost you extra laps after practice."

"But, Coach, she knocked me down over there—"

Alan cut her off impatiently. "I don't want to hear it.

44

You'll run extra laps. No throwing the ball." He turned to Wendy. "Are you all right?"

Wendy nodded, wiping at a tear, and Dawn thought she detected just the slightest smile as she looked past the coach toward Karin.

Karin glared at her, looked around at the rest of the team, and started walking toward the gym.

"Hey, where are you going?" Dawn called, running after her.

"Home!" Karin responded angrily. "She started that, and I'm not running any stupid laps, that's for sure!"

Dawn stared in dismay as Karin walked even faster and then ran from the practice field.

5
Diamond Defense

Dawn pushed open the door at White's Cafe and paused for a few seconds to let the air-conditioning wash over her. Her eyes adjusted to the interior light and she spoted Nathan, Troy, and a couple of juniors from the high school soccer team sitting in a corner booth.

Nathan got up and walked over to meet her as she took a couple of steps inside. She hoped her face wasn't as flushed as she felt. She mustered her courage and greeted him with a shy smile.

"Hi," Nathan said, with a pleased smile. "Thought maybe you forgot about it. We got here twenty minutes ago."

"Sorry," she said as he motioned toward a booth. They slid in on opposite sides. "Our first practice went longer than I expected. Our new coaches are going to be tough, but maybe we'll start winning some games. How's your team looking?"

"Okay, I think," he said, brushing a hand over his curly brown hair. "You want a Coke or something?"

At her nod, Nathan walked over to the counter where Mr. White, the owner, took the order. Dawn watched him and felt her heart pounding. He was cute. No doubt about it. His curly hair accented a bronzed face and bright blue eyes. He wasn't very tall, but he looked tall because of his athletic build. She had wanted to go out with him for months—ever since he'd talked with her for about fifteen minutes during a church sleigh ride last January. Now they were together, and she didn't know what to say or do.

She looked up expectantly as he started back toward her with two Cokes. He placed the drinks on the table and slipped back into the booth.

"How's your nose feeling?" he asked after they each took a sip. "Looks pretty good. In fact, you look great!"

Dawn blushed and took another sip before replying.

"Thanks. My nose doesn't even feel tender today. It's the rest of me that's stiff and sore after soccer practice."

He laughed. "I felt that way last week at this time. Seems like no matter how much you think you're ready to go, you find out the truth in a hurry once practice begins. I think the coaches have special exercises to make *sure* that you feel miserable for a couple days."

She giggled. "Keeps you humble."

"For sure. Well, you ready for your last year in junior high? I was a little nervous about high school, but the guys on the soccer team have made Troy and me feel welcome."

"I'm ready. This was going to be my year to take it easy, but now I've got soccer AND I'm going to help on the church's youth forum."

Nathan looked interested. "Haven't heard about it. Is that something new this year?"

"I thought all the kids in the church knew about it. Rev Steve set it up for grades nine through twelve instead of just the high schoolers. It started last Sunday, but only eight kids came."

"Bummer, huh," he said, gulping at his pop.

"Actually, it was pretty good. He's going to let us run it ourselves, and we're going to get some sort of special project going. Maybe something on hunger. Did you know there are big sections of the United States where people are starving? It's just like Africa, only it's right here. . . ." She paused. "Sorry. I get a little carried away."

He laughed. "Must be better than what we've had before. I was thinking about staying out of senior high Sunday school class. Maybe I should take a second look."

"Oh, would you? I mean . . ." she paused, embarrassed again. "I told Rev Steve I would try to recruit some more kids. So far, you're it."

"You really think it's good, huh?"

"Well . . . yeah. But we need more kids and some ideas." She gave him an inviting smile. "Besides, I'd really like it if you were there."

He finished his Coke and contemplated the empty glass before nodding. "I'll think about it."

"Okay." Dawn glanced at her watch and gulped the rest of her drink. "I've got to get home for supper."

"I'll walk you," Nathan said, sliding out of the booth. "That is . . . if it's all right with you." He reached out to her and helped her from the booth, and she felt a small electric charge go through her fingertips as his hand touched hers. She glanced at him to see if he felt it, too. If he did, his face didn't show it.

"Y-yes," she stammered, getting up. "I'd like that."

"Good. Maybe we can get together again before school gets started." He smiled warmly, and Dawn wondered why her knees felt so shaky.

Dawn arrived early at practice the next day and was surprised to meet Karin coming out of the gym, carrying her gym bag, as she was going in.

48

"Hi," she said as Karin gave her a pained look. "What's up?"

"Came to get my stuff. I'm not staying."

"You going to Academy?"

Karin nodded. "Yeah. I'd be miserable here with . . . with the way things are with Wendy. You know?"

Dawn half-nodded.

"I think I'll like it at Academy. My dad talked to their coach and their principal last night, and they're both happy to have me. The coach said they need a right winger who can score."

Dawn started to say something but couldn't seem to get the words out. She stared down at her feet, then looked back up and spoke quickly.

"Look, if you get over there and you're not happy, I hope you'll come back. The other girls on the team —we'll work on Wendy. You could fit in before too long. I just know it."

Karin toed the ground and gripped her gym bag tightly. "Maybe. I think I just need a year to get ready for high school, and I don't need any hassles from some-one like Wendy while I'm doing it."

"You coming back to North Park High, then?"

"I told my dad I wanted to," she answered. "Course, maybe I'll really like it over there and want to stay. Who knows?"

"Sure, who knows?" Dawn said half-heartedly. She'd never remembered anyone who had left North Park for Academy and then returned. They always stayed. Suddenly she felt like crying, and she didn't know why. She still barely knew Karin. "Karin," she said. "I-I wish you wouldn't go. I-we—really like you." She reached over and gave her a little hug, which Karin returned.

"Thanks, but I've got to. It's not like I'm moving away, you know." She smiled at Dawn. "I'll still see you around town and in church. Right?"

"Right." Dawn forced a smile. "Then, after you spend a year getting your scoring down, you can come back here and help our high school team win the state championship."

"So, you're going over to Academy, huh?" a haughty voice interrupted. Wendy. They hadn't seen her round the corner, so they didn't know how long she'd been listening. "It's a second-rate team, but you'll probably like it."

"We'll see," Karin said calmly. "At least I won't have to put up with someone who thinks she can win games by herself. As far as scoring goes, I'll just do my best."

"No one in the league is going to outscore me this year, especially you!" Wendy exclaimed.

Karin glared at her, then smiled. "Maybe," she said. She turned and laid a hand on Dawn's shoulder. "Hope *you* have a good season," she said. "Maybe I can give you a call sometime?"

Dawn nodded, looking miserably from Karin to Wendy and back again. *Why couldn't it be Wendy walking away to Academy and Karin staying?* she thought. *How come, God? It isn't fair.*

As Wendy pushed past her into the gym, Dawn turned her back and waved good-bye to Karin.

By the third day of practice, three things were apparent: everyone was upset with Wendy for driving Karin away, Wendy was better than ever at scoring, and Dawn was showing signs of becoming a pretty decent defensive player.

She was still having problems with Wendy, especially when Wendy slipped past the halfbacks and made her move toward the goal. When Dawn gave in to the urge to charge the ball, Wendy would make a good fake and then either power a shot past her or finesse one through before Dawn could scramble back into position.

About halfway through practice, the coach called the goalie, the fullbacks, and the center halfback together.

"We're going to try a new defense," he said. "You set up in a diamond pattern. If the ball is coming straight down the middle, then Trini is the top point and the left and right fullbacks are the side points. The bottom point is Dawn at her sweeper spot." He made a circular motion with his arms.

"Each of you is responsible for a big circle around yourself—maybe fifteen or twenty feet on each side. It's your zone. If the ball is in your zone, you go after it. Once it's out of your zone, the next person in the diamond has to pick it up, depending on where the ball is." He pointed at Trini Dahl, the midfielder who played directly in front of Dawn. "She's the stopper. When the ball starts down the center of the field, Trini has the first responsibility. If it goes past her to her left, then Jeannie becomes the top point of the diamond, Trini and Dawn are covering the sides."

He walked over to Jeannie Delavane at the right wing defender spot.

"Now Jeannie is the point," he called. "Dawn is the right side of the diamond, and Ginger is way back." He waved back toward Ginger Pascoe, the left fullback. "And Beth is always shifting in goal, but she's got three people between her and the ball who are helping on defense."

The girls looked around at where they were positioned.

Alan continued his explanation. "You're always in a diamond, so you've almost always got three people in position to stop the girl with the ball and a fourth person at the bottom point who can intercept long passes and protect the weak side. As the ball moves, a new defensive player picks it up, and the other one drops back to help protect the goal. It always keeps three defenders plus the goalie in front of the girl with the ball."

He dribbled the ball toward them. Trini challenged it, and he shifted to his left. Immediately Jeannie went to challenge the ball, and Dawn shifted down closer to the goal, staying in her general area. He brought the ball all the way back around and tried to challenge between Dawn and Ginger.

Ginger stepped wide and Dawn picked up the shot, stopped it neatly with her right foot, and kicked it over to Jeannie.

"Good." Alan clapped his hands and nodded. "You see how it works?"

The girls nodded, pleased with themselves.

"Once you get into the habit of shifting and covering your area, you'll find you can make stops like Dawn just did almost every time. We've got to make them work hard for every goal, and the diamond zone defense is a great way to do it. On top of that, when you're not the one challenging the ball, you can sort of rest. It keeps you fresher for later in the game."

Alan signaled to Wendy and Carla to come.

"I want you two to work the ball against this defense," he said. "And go hard. I want to see if you can get it inside."

He blew his whistle, and Carla started the ball with Trini shifting to challenge. Carla quickly kicked it over to Wendy, who eased the ball to her right, into Ginger's zone. Ginger made her move to cover, and Dawn started sliding to the side. Suddenly Wendy stepped across the ball, moved it with her left foot between Dawn and Ginger, and dribbled quickly toward Dawn's right.

Caught off guard, Dawn backpeddled to her right to cut off the attack. Before she could get set, Wendy stopped and smacked the ball firmly past Dawn's left.

The shot was high and smooth, rising quickly past the outstretched hands of the goalie and into the net. Wendy half-smirked and returned to the middle of the field as Beth retrieved the ball in disgust. Dawn scuffed at the ground and hung her head. She'd been suckered for sure. Wendy's goal looked too easy.

She glanced toward Alan, who was shaking his head.

"Forget about her feet; watch her eyes!"

Dawn looked up at the sound of a familiar voice. There was Rev Steve standing along the far sideline. She paused to let his words sink in, then nodded. He clapped his hands together as the whistle blew. Wendy immediately picked up a pass and started to move downfield.

Dawn set herself and watched the flow of the play, observing where her teammates were and where she needed to be. She checked back over her shoulder and gave a thumbs-up sign to Beth in goal. Then she shifted slightly as Wendy veered away from the sideline and came straight toward her position in the center of the field. Wendy bore down on her with the ball and made a little fake to her left. But instead of jumping off in that direction, Dawn held her ground and watched Wendy's eyes.

She saw Wendy's brief glance toward the right corner of the goal, even as she dribbled left, and Dawn dropped back two steps. At that precise second, Wendy spun around and attempted her shot—to the right.

Quickly Dawn lunged with her left leg and caught the full impact of the shot on her thigh. It stung like crazy, but she bit down on her lip, blinked away a tear, and hurried to gain control of the ball. Before Wendy could react, Dawn had booted the ball long and hard back upfield, out of scoring position. The coach blew his whistle and signaled for the team to join him.

"Nice stop, Dawn," Beth said as she loped up from

her goalie's position. "If you had missed that, it would've gone in for sure. I was moving the opposite direction."

"Thanks." Dawn smiled.

"Hey! Lucky stop!" Wendy shouted as she ran past them.

"Yeah, hey, thanks," Dawn muttered.

"Don't let Miss Wonderful bug you," Beth said, patting Dawn on the shoulder. "Does her good to get stuffed once in a while."

"I know," Dawn laughed. "Makes her so nice and humble, right?"

Dawn glanced at the sidelines and grinned as Rev Steve gave her the high sign. She waved back and then hurried to join the rest of the team as they gathered around the coach at the center of the field.

6
New Directions

"Have a chair," Alan said, gesturing toward the turf.

The girls dropped down onto the field, panting and wiping the sweat from their faces.

He glanced around the circle. "Three days of practice in, and we're not looking too bad. You're starting to make your passes and you're getting more accurate with your longer kicks. I'm still a little concerned about our overall defense, but I think we'll be okay if we remember to help each other out.

"Good stop down there just now, Dawn," he said, pointing in her direction. "That's the kind of defense our fullbacks have to play to help the keeper. If we do, we're going to win a lot of games, I guarantee you."

Susan stepped forward with a clipboard in her hand. "Anyone have any bad aches or pains?" she asked, glancing at the roster sheet attached to the board. "Carla, how's the blister on your left foot?"

"Better," Carla responded. She was lying on her back, her hands across her eyes to keep out the sun. "I put some ointment on today and wrapped it before practice."

"Good. Anyone else with anything major? If you

have bruises, those will get better, but if your muscles are bothering you—especially in your thighs and calves—I need to know so we can be sure it isn't anything serious."

No one spoke.

"Well, great." She looked toward Alan. "We must not be working these girls hard enough. They all feel okay."

The team erupted into a chorus of moans and groans.

"All right, all right," Alan said, waving his hands for quiet. "I don't suppose anyone would object if we stopped practice fifteen minutes early today. Three straight days in this heat is starting to get to me, too. Let's call it a day." The girls cheered, and then Alan waved for silence once again.

"Many of you know Rev Steve Sobasky, who helps with the guys' team. Well, he thought we'd been working hard, too, so he brought us a treat. Enjoy! See you all at practice tomorrow."

The girls ambled over to the sidelines, where Rev Steve stood with a couple boxes of ice cream bars.

He greeted Dawn with a smile, and handed her a stick.

"Not bad defense down there, Miss Davis. You must be taking lessons from a pro."

Dawn grinned. "Thanks. My pro's a real slavedriver, you know."

"I've heard that about him," Rev Steve answered. "But seriously, that was a good stop. The girl who was driving on you made a great fake, too. From my angle it looked like she was going to go the other way. I was proud of you for not coming out of position to challenge her too soon. Your goalie was way out of position."

"She told me," Dawn said. "I remembered to watch Wendy's eyes, and I saw her glance the other way even when she moved to her left. That's why I dropped off a little and looked for the shot to the right."

"Good. We'll work more on that on Saturday." He finished up his ice cream and stood. "Well, I've got to get over to the church and prepare for this evening's services. You having any luck rounding up kids for Sunday?"

"I've got at least two." Dawn stopped and looked past the minister toward two boys walking their direction. Nathan and Troy. "Maybe three."

Rev Steve glanced over his shoulder, saw the boys, and smiled. "Well, I hope so." He turned away. "See you in a couple days." Dawn waited until the boys reached her.

"How's practice?" Nathan said in greeting.

"Good, I think. We've been working pretty hard, but I don't feel too bad. How come you guys are off early?"

"Coach thought it was too hot to go long today," Troy answered. We finished about half an hour ago."

"Looks like you've been taking a few shots," Nathan said, pointing to a black-and-blue mark on Dawn's left leg, just above her knee.

She grimaced. "Don't remind me. By Friday, I'll probably be black-and-blue from head to toe."

"Well, at least your face is better," Nathan said quickly. "You look great."

"When do you guys have your first game?" asked Dawn, changing the subject.

"Next Tuesday. We play Rosemount."

"Gee, tough team right off," Dawn sympathized. "We don't play till a week from Monday—at Academy."

"That's a tough one, too," Troy said as they approached the gym.

"I know. Hope I can come over and watch you play. It's kind of hard to get away from practice, but at least none of your games are on the same nights as ours."

"Well, I've got to get going. See you around." Troy waved and left.

Nathan turned to Dawn. "Uh, would you mind if I hung around and walked you home?"

"Sure," she said, "if you don't mind waiting. It'll be fifteen or twenty minutes."

"No problem," Nathan said. "I'll mess around out here."

Dawn smiled. "Okay. I'll hurry." Suddenly she didn't feel at all tired. She hummed happily as she showered and changed in record time. When she came back out of the gym, Nathan was banging the ball off the wall and fielding his own kicks.

"Got time for a Coke or something?" he asked. "We can stop over at the Huddle."

The Huddle was a popular neighborhood cafe just a few blocks from the schools. Whenever the kids weren't down at White's, they were usually at the Huddle instead.

Nathan and Dawn walked slowly in the late afternoon heat, talking about soccer and school. They reached the Huddle and found a booth in the corner.

"So, how's your recruiting for the forum going?" he asked.

Dawn shook her head. "Slowly, I'm afraid. Beth Merriman said she'd give it a try, and Tricia—the midfielder who's Wendy's friend—said she might come. Counting the eight of us who were there last week, that'll make ten."

"Make it eleven," Nathan corrected. "I'll give it a try. But if it turns out to be another 'sit around and stare at each other' session like we had last year, I'll pass."

"Hey, I know it's going to be good. We got so involved last week that we hardly knew where the hour went!" In her enthusiasm, Dawn reached across the table and grabbed his hand to emphasize her point.

58

Then she stopped and pulled it away, feeling a flush of embarrassment wash over her face. "Sorry."

But Nathan grabbed her hand before she could pull it away. "Hey," he said, with a twinkle in his eye. "If this forum thing can get you to hold hands with me, I'm all for it. I'll just say 'forum,' and you'll take my hand." A voice at their side interrupted him.

"Who had the root beer float?"

Nathan nodded toward Dawn, whose face was turning bright crimson. The waitress plunked the glasses down impatiently, and Dawn began drinking furiously. Then, trying to suppress a grin, she put both hands over her face in embarrassment.

Nathan waited a few seconds before speaking. "Is she gone?"

Dawn nodded.

"Good. Now, where were we?" He paused as if thinking, then slapped his hand down on the table, palm up, and said firmly, "Forum."

They both collapsed in laughter as the waitress hurried by with another order and gave them an odd stare.

By Saturday Dawn had worked out the kinks from the first full week of practice. She arrived early at the little soccer field at Hyde Park for her seven o'clock meeting with Rev Steve. For the first time in ten days, the heat had dissipated, and the early morning was refreshingly cool.

The minister hadn't arrived, so Dawn settled under a tree and leaned back, studying the sky and the leaves moving gently in the early morning breeze. She closed her eyes for a few seconds, thinking how Nathan had met her after practice again yesterday and walked her home.

"All because of a stupid soccer ball," she said aloud.

"What stupid soccer ball?"

Dawn jumped and sat up straight. Karin was standing in front of her, a soccer ball tucked under one arm.

"Oh, hi," Dawn said. "What're you doing here?"

"Just came by to do some work. I didn't expect to find anyone else around so early. Are you all right?"

Dawn laughed. "I'm fine. Rev Steve is meeting me here to help me out with some defensive plays."

"So, is that the stupid soccer ball you were muttering about?"

"Nah. I was just thinking about getting bashed in the face a couple weeks ago. Believe it or not, it's gotten me acquainted with Nathan Hall."

"Nathan? I don't know him very well, but I've certainly noticed him."

"He's the one who hit me with the ball. I really like him."

"Well, I'd *hope* so!" Karin exclaimed. "You'd be crazy not to. If you're not interested, let me know."

"Sorry," Dawn said. "He's taken."

Karin smiled. "Well, I'd settle for that other guy I always see him with."

"Troy?"

"Yeah, Troy." Karin looked away. "Probably not much chance of meeting him, either, now that I'm over at Academy."

Dawn stood up and brushed the grass off her shorts and socks. "So, how *is* Academy? Have you gotten started with soccer?"

"Seems okay. The coach is nice. Once we get into classes next week, I'm sure I'll like it. How's your practice been going?"

"Pretty good. I think I'm playing defense well, but I need a lot of work." She pointed toward the parking lot as a red station wagon pulled up. "There's Rev Steve now. He used to play center fullback in college."

Karin looked interested. "I didn't know that. I

haven't talked with him much." She watched the minister get out of his car. "Well, I'd better get moving. I'll work on my shots over there," she said, pointing to the goal at the far end of the park, "and you guys can work over here, if that's okay with you. See ya."

"Hey," Dawn called after her. "You doing anything tomorrow?"

"Hadn't really thought about it. Why?"

"I was just thinking you might want to come to Sunday school." Dawn held up a hand to stop Karin's refusal. "It's a special youth forum. Rev Steve is working with us to develop a special project—helping to feed hungry people or something. I wish you'd come."

Karin shrugged. "I'll think about it."

Dawn beamed. "Great." She waved as Karin left, and then turned herself to greet Rev Steve as he hurried up.

"Sorry to keep you waiting," he panted. "Had to run a couple of errands downtown, and they took longer than I expected. Who's that?" He gestured toward Karin.

"Karin Gardner. She goes to our church . . . sometimes. They're pretty new in North Park. She came to the junior high last spring, but now she's going to Academy."

"Too bad," Rev Steve said as he watched her set up and kick a shot into the net. "Looks like she has a pretty good touch."

"No kidding!" Dawn answered. "I thought we'd be unbeatable this year with Karin and Wendy, but it didn't take Wendy long to get her out of here." Dawn related the Monday incident that had led to Karin's decision to transfer.

Rev Steve frowned. "Seems like it has to be something deeper than that," he commented, watching Karin neatly dribble the ball back and forth across the field.

"Maybe," said Dawn. "They kind of got into it last spring, and Karin was already thinking of transferring. Last Monday just made it happen sooner. They way Wendy's been acting, we're lucky we even have a team."

"What do you mean?" he asked.

"Oh, you now. She thinks she's so much better than the rest of us—and she is really good. I just wish she could be a little nicer. She never has a good word about anyone except herself. It gets a little tiring."

"I would think so. Anyone ever try to sit down and talk with her about it?"

"No one can stand to be around her. We just put up with her bragging and do the best we can. Of course, the coach just loves her because she *is* a good shooter. And her dad helped him get the job."

"Seriously?"

"Well, that's the talk. Alan seems like a pretty good coach, but he's going to teach, too. Everyone thinks he got both jobs because Wendy's dad put in a good word for him. It's easy for us to see that she can do no wrong as far as Alan is concerned, so he probably owes her dad a favor."

Rev Steve just looked intently at her, and Dawn realized how she must have come across.

"Sorry," she said. "Guess I sound pretty mean myself, huh?"

He smiled.

"I think Karin got forced out, that's all, and Wendy's been lording it over us ever since. Why do people have to be that way?"

"Good question," he replied. "Maybe she needs someone who will care enough about her to help her change. But let's worry about Wendy another time. Right now, I want you to worry about stopping shots and getting the ball up where Wendy has a chance to score. Like it

62

or not, she's going to be the one to put the ball into the net for the Polars. And," he added dramatically, "Dawn Davis is going to be the one to keep the ball out of the Polars' nets. Okay?"

"Okay," she said. He held out a hand and she slapped it high five fashion.

Down the field, Karin had stopped and was staring at the duo, her foot resting on top of her own soccer ball.

7
Issues and Actions

"Do you know that tonight 300 million children will go to bed hungry?" Rev Steve glanced around the room at the twelve teenagers sitting with him. "Do you know that this year alone, 20 million people are going to die from hunger or hunger-related diseases? It's hard to imagine that as we sit here with full stomachs in a nice room. But it's true."

"But what can we do about it?" Nathan asked. "We're twelve kids in the middle of America."

"Aha. I thought you'd never ask," Rev Steve said quickly. The kids broke into nervous laughter. "You may just be twelve kids in the middle of America, but there are things you can do." He rifled through a pile of papers in front of him and pulled out a newspaper clipping.

"Here's a story about some kids in New York City who got their community to share what they had so that others in the world could eat. The group was larger than ours, it's true, but they also were living in an area where people had traditionally not shown a lot of love and compassion for other human beings." He slapped the clipping for emphasis. "Do you know that by the time they were finished, they had gathered together twenty tons—that's *tons*—of food to send to starving people. Kids CAN get things done."

"Okay, I think all of us would like to help keep other kids from starving," Dawn said. "But where would we start? What do we do first?"

"What you do first is become as familiar as you can with the world food situation, and then start on a project that you know is within your reach. Twelve kids can't solve the world food problem, but maybe, just maybe, twelve kids can get a project off the ground to provide enough food for ghetto families in a nearby city.

"I'm not talking about North Park," Rev Steve added. "North Park doesn't have any starving people. But St. Louis does; Chicago does; Minneapolis does; Portland does; Los Angeles does. Maybe something you do here can help feed a hungry child in one of those cities." He stopped and waited for a response.

"I wonder how much we'd have to get in order to help," Bob said aloud, almost as if talking to himself.

"Maybe tons—at least tons," Monica answered. "Do you think we could raise tons, like those kids in New York did?"

They began talking quietly among themselves, and Rev Steve sat back and smiled.

"Now," he interrupted. "I think this youth forum is off to a good start. You spend some time talking over ideas and bring me back a plan for next week. It's about time for St. Peter's Church to start setting an example for others around here, and it's going to start with this group. Right here. Right now."

The kids broke into cheers. Dawn glanced at her mentor, and he responded with a smile and a thumbs up sign. She responded with "thumbs up" of her own, then stopped as she saw Rev Steve looking past her at the doorway. Dawn turned. Standing in the doorway was Karin. She jumped up and went to greet her.

"Hi," she said, grabbing Karin by the arm and pulling her into the room. "Hey, everyone do you know Karin? Karin Gardner. She's new in our church. Come on," she continued, leading Karin to the circle. "We're working on a project to help feed hungry people, and we need your help."

She pulled a chair up next to hers for Karin, and then she turned to give another "thumbs up" to Rev Steve. Something exciting was happening here, and Dawn was glad to be part of it.

Much to everyone's relief, school opened on a cool day. After getting through the first-hour jitters, Dawn settled into the reality of a hard workload.

Right after lunch, she entered her world affairs class and found her soccer coach standing at the podium. She greeted him shyly and settled into a third-row seat, while Alan beamed at her.

Carla slipped into a seat directly behind Dawn and tapped her on the shoulder. "Did you know he was teaching this?"

"No way," Dawn said, half-turning. "Do you suppose he knows anything about teaching at all?"

"Probably not," Carla answered. "Remember, he just got this job in the first place 'cause he sucked up to Wendy's old man. They had to find some class to stick him in, and here he is. Lucky us, huh?"

"Yeah, really," Dawn replied, looking glumly at her desk.

The bell rang, and the coach shuffled nervously to the blackboard where he had already written WORLD AFFAIRS, MR. YOUNG in large letters. Pointing to the board, he cleared his throat and nodded. "This is the class, and that's me—that's my name, I mean, even though I am."

The students laughed appreciatively, and he grinned.

"Well," he continued, "we're about to make history here. I'm in my first classroom, and you're my first guineau pi—I mean, pupils.

"I don't know what you expect out of a World Affairs class, but let's find out." He pointed to Tony Dominguez, who had come in just at the bell and settled in the last seat available in the front row. "What do you think?"

"Why me?" Tony answered, looking both startled and defiant.

"Why not? You must have some idea of what world affairs means."

Tony sat up straighter and scratched his head. "I dunno," he finally replied. "Could be anything, I guess. Maybe a couple countries fighting each other?"

"Sure, maybe," Alan answered. "But why should we care if a couple of backward nations in Latin America are having problems? What's it to us, anyway?"

The room grew silent at the teacher's obvious reference to Tony's heritage. Dawn could see Tony's face flush.

"My folks came from Mexico," he said angrily. "You better watch who you're . . . ,"

"Calling backward," Alan finished, cutting him off quickly and striding to the board to jerk down a map of the world. "Exactly." He spoke firmly. "Look at this map, all of you!" his voice was riveting, and everyone in the room gazed at the colorful map he had unrolled. "Right here we've got the whole world. One neat little package, isn't it? Well, let me tell you, ladies and gentlemen, the world may be little, but it isn't neat! It's not neat at all."

He took a few steps in front of the map, then swung

around and rapped it with his hand. "Latin America. Every nation is either fighting with its next door neighbor, or it's so divided that everyone within the nation is fighting with his *own* neighbor." He swung his hand across the Atlantic Ocean and rapped again. "The Middle East. People are blowing each other away by the hundreds every day, and some of the leaders are threatening to bomb Europe *and* the United States."

He took a deep breath. The silence in the room was almost deafening. Then he swung his hand again, this time across the broad expanse of colors making up the Asian nations. "The Orient. A couple of billion—that's B as in starving babies, billion—people who are looking at which nation they might need to start a war with so that they can maybe capture enough rice for next month's meals." He pulled at the bottom of the map and let it spring back up with a snap. Then he took a couple of steps and stopped in front of Tony's desk.

"So you see, friends, the world's all rolled up in a neat little package, but it's not neat! And, let me tell you that what happens in a Latin American nation—" he stopped and flashed a smile at Tony, "or in a remote Middle East village, *or* in a rice paddy in China is going to mean everything in the world to you and me and this nation.

"When the United States sends money to a starving nation to help feed the people, and then that money gets turned into guns and bullets, it's not neat! When a teenager like you sees his mother or father killed by a bullet that came indirectly from the United States, he doesn't stop to think that we intended to send food. All he remembers is where the bullet came from.

"Like it or not, this world is tied together. So what happens in world affairs affects me," he paused and barely breathed out the next words, "and it affects *you* . . . *every one of you.*"

Dawn hardly dared look around the room, but she peeked from the corner of her eye and saw virtually everyone giving full attention to the new young teacher. Alan walked across in front of his desk and leaned against it.

"Now," he said. "Let me tell you what we'll be doing in this class in the weeks ahead."

When the bell rang, signaling the class period's end, some of the class members actually groaned in disgust. Dawn stared admiringly at her new teacher.

"Pretty good, huh!" It was Carla.

Dawn nodded. "Yeah." She glanced at the floor.

"I know," Carla said. "I feel like a jerk for saying what I did earlier. If he can coach half as good as he teaches, we'll win the championship for sure." They laughed together and hurried toward their lockers.

As the week progressed, school got harder, Alan's class stayed interesting, and soccer practice got tougher. The opening game was the following Monday at Academy, followed by a Thursday match on their home field against Brownsville.

Both Alan and Susan were sharp with the girls when they made bad passes or shots or lapses in defense. By Friday, everyone was looking forward to a weekend off, and Dawn and her teammates registered shock and dismay when Alan announced a "match conditions" scrimmage to close out the week's tough practice schedule.

"You've got all weekend to rest up after this. I need to know if you're ready or not," he responded when they erupted in a chorus of groans. "I'm putting our best defenders on the field against our best attackers, and we'll see what happens. This is my way of determining who starts on Monday."

Still grumbling, the girls made their way into position as Susan read off the lineups.

Dawn stared ahead at the center of the field. Lining up at forward were Carla, Wendy, Tricia, and Dotty Washington, who was turning out to be a surprisingly strong center. Dawn glanced back to see if Beth was set.

"Remember the diamond!" she shouted, as Alan blew his whistle and put the ball into play at midfield.

Immediately Wendy took control of the ball and went on the attack, racing past Allison and pushing a quick pass down the line to Carla. Carla controlled the pass, dribbled a couple of yards, and then laid the ball off to Wendy as she broke into the midst of the halfbacks.

"Here she comes!" Dawn shouted as Wendy scooted to the open space between Trini and Becka Jones, the left halfback. Becka tried to slide tackle the ball, missed badly, and scrambled to her feet as Wendy charged on, dribbling quickly toward Dawn's center fullback position.

"Trini, goal side, pick her up!" she yelled, "I've got back!" Dawn dropped back three paces into the bottom of the diamond zone and then jockeyed for position, trying to force Wendy away from the danger area or stop the shot—whatever was necessary. She stared at Wendy's face, but saw nothing but determination.

"Take the far post," she shouted over her shoulder. Beth dropped back to cover Dawn's left and prepare for the shot. Just as it looked like a collision was inevitable, Wendy half-skidded to a stop. She faked to her left and then kicked the ball off the outside of her own right foot just to Dawn's left as Dawn jumped to the right.

Too late, Dawn tried to backpeddle to the loose ball as Wendy sprinted into the little gap between Dawn and the left fullback, Ginger Pascoe. Now Ginger was closing in from the left side, Dawn was coming back from the right, and Beth was blocking the path directly in front of Wendy.

70

"Now we've got you trapped," Dawn muttered aloud, pleased that she had cut off the angle of the shot and forced Wendy into a vise. But three yards in front of Beth, Wendy stopped and chopped down hard at the ball with her instep. A chunk of sod came up with the ball, which exploded upward from the force of the shot, going straight up and at least six feet over Beth's outstretched arms.

"Oh, no!" Dawn exclaimed. "I don't believe it!"

The ball continued its upward path and almost as suddenly headed back down, dropping neatly into the little space just in front of the net and bouncing in for the goal. Dawn shook her head in grudging respect, as Beth disgustedly walked back to dig out the ball and Wendy jogged back upfield.

"Nice shot!" Dawn called after her.

Wendy waved casually over her shoulder, and Carla gave Dawn a sympathetic shrug before trotting back upfield.

"Sometimes she's so good she's scary," Beth said as she dropped the ball at Dawn's feet. "If only she'd try to be civilized once in a while."

"Yeah," Dawn answered, dropping the ball and kicking it hard toward the center of the field, "if only." *Come on, God,* she thought. *You can help make Wendy be a better person, can't You? If You can make her that good of an athlete, You can make her a good person, too.* She dropped back into her defensive space to get ready for more.

After half an hour of hard play, Alan blew his whistle and called the team to the center of the field.

"Okay," he said with a satisfied sound in his voice. "We're as ready as we can hope to be for an opener. We've got someone who can score and we've got a respectable defense. If we play the kind of game I know we can play, we're going to get off to a good start Monday at Melrose Academy. Am I right?"

"Right!" the team shouted in unison, clapping hard.

"All right, then." He held out his right hand, palm up, and the girls crowded around to stack their hands together on top of his. "What do you say, Polars? You ready?"

"Yeah!" they shouted.

"Go get 'em, Polars," Tricia cried.

They held their hands tightly together, counted to three and shouted "Polars!" then broke out of the huddle and into a spontaneous lap around the field. Even Wendy joined in, and the girls were shouting and laughing as they ran past the coaches and on into the gym.

"I'm psyched," Dawn said to Carla as they emerged from the locker with gym bags in hand. "I know Wendy made our defense look pretty bad a couple of times, but I think we did okay on her, too. The last couple of times she didn't even get a shot away. And if we can stop *her*, we can definitely stop Academy." She paused. "Even Karin, I think."

"That's it, be decisive," Carla chided.

Dawn gave her a little shove. As they crossed the street leading toward Dawn's house, Carla nudged Dawn in the side and pointed up the street. Two figures were rapidly moving their way.

"This has to be more than a coincidence," she said with a sigh, as Dawn waved cheerily to Nathan and Troy. "It *must* be love; what else would make a person take the eighteen-block route home?"

"Come off it," Dawn said, blushing. "It's not that much out of his way."

"If it were any more out of his way, he'd be in the next city," Carla laughed. "But don't worry, your love life's a secret with me."

They stopped giggling as the two boys drew near.

"Hi," Nathan began. "Long time, no see."

Dawn grinned. They had met the night before on her way home from practice, too. And on Tuesday night he'd called her after their opening game against Rosemount—a 2-1 win for the Polars in which he'd scored the winning goal.

"I hear you're the hero," Carla said. "Don't you know sophomores aren't supposed to be good enough to score winning goals?"

Nathan smiled. "Troy and I figure somebody's got to change all that bunk. Right?"

"Right," Carla answered, holding out her hand palm up and receiving a hand slap from Nathan in response.

"So, how's your own team?"

"Good. We're ready to win," Dawn said. "If we don't, I think the coach'll just die."

"Not to mention Wendy," Carla chimed in.

"How *is* good old Wendy?" Troy asked. "Still sure she's the answer to everyone's dreams?"

"Sort of," Dawn said. "She *is* pretty good, you know."

"Too bad she's got such a big head," Troy replied. "Otherwise she's kind of cute."

"What about us?" Carla said indignantly. "Aren't we kind of cute, too?"

"Oh, sure," Troy stammered. "You guys are cute, too. Really!" He looked quickly to Nathan for support. "Tell 'em, Nathan," he said. "They're cute, right?"

Nathan glanced over at Carla, then swung his gaze back to Dawn. "Absolutely."

He said it with such sincerity that both Troy and Carla glanced quickly in his direction.

"Well, um . . . ," Carla said to no one in particular. "Listen, Dawn, I've got to get home." She sidestepped toward Troy and nudged him with her elbow. "Troy.

You heading my way? This is where Dawn and I usually split up."

"Oh!" Troy was startled by Carla's nudge. "Oh, sure.
Maybe I can walk with you?"

"Dawn?" Carla spoke louder, and Dawn shook her
head slightly.

"Okay," Dawn replied.

"Okay, what?" Carla answered.

"What did you say?" Dawn asked, turning to look
directly at her friend.

Carla snickered. "Nothing. I've got to get going. See
you sometime tomorrow." She grabbed Troy's elbow
and steered him away. " 'Bye, Nathan. Hope you can
take time to walk Dawn home."

"Huh?" Nathan said, appearing confused. "Oh. 'Bye,
Carla." He turned to Troy. "Hey, look, why don't you
walk along with Carla. She lives over your way."
Before Troy could say anything, he continued. "I'll
walk Dawn home. It's sort of on my way, anyway."

"Right. So's the moon," Carla said.

"What?" Nathan replied.

"I said I better get going or it's going to be noon." She
smirked and grabbed Troy's arm, pulling him along.
"Come on," she added loudly. "I don't want anyone
saying I stood in the way of true love."

Carla and Troy started off, and Nathan looked in
their direction. "I like Carla," he said, "but sometimes
she doesn't make any sense. You know?"

"Yeah, I guess," Dawn said. "You really going to
walk me home?"

"If you want. I'd like to."

"Sure," she said. "It's kind of on your way, isn't it?"

"Kind of." He held out his hand to her, and they
started slowly up the street toward her house.

In the distance, Dawn heard Carla laugh. "The
moon!" she called. "I said, the moon!"

8
Surprise Partner

The mid-afternoon sun was bright and warm as Dawn and her teammates trotted onto the field. They were wearing new uniforms of blue, trimmed in silver, and Dawn felt a surge of pride as a crowd of her classmates erupted in a cheer.

"Great uniforms!" shouted a voice from the sidelines where the North Park kids were gathered in a cluster.

"We do look pretty good in these, you know," Dawn said to Carla, as they formed into ranks for calisthentics. "I'm surprised the budget allowed for them."

"The school didn't pay for them," Wendy said from behind them.

"How do you know?" Dawn challenged her.

" 'Cause my dad did, that's how I know."

"Oh, brother," Carla puffed as she dropped down and began stretching her legs in a hurdler's position.

But Dawn brightened. "Hey, I think it's great! Tell him we really appreciate it, okay?"

Wendy gave her an inquisitive glance and finally a small smile. "Sure," she said. "I think he'll be glad to hear that." She got up from her own stretching position and began jogging slowly around the field.

"What's with you?" Carla said with dismay.

"Nothing. I was going to say something mean, but why do that when I really do like the uniforms? I know her dad just got them so he could get some good pictures of Wendy in action, but so what? We all got something nice out of the deal, right?"

Carla ran her hand along the side of the uniform and nodded. "Yeah. I guess I like them, too. Now, if they'll only help us win, I'll absolutely love them. Promise."

"I think great defense and a good offense is what we'll need to help us win. Rev Steve told me to worry about those two things and nothing else, and we'll win for sure. Simple, huh?"

A roar from the large crowd of Academy kids on the far sideline signaled the arrival of their team. Dawn and Carla stopped exercising and watched as twenty-five girls in bright red-and-blue uniforms ran onto the field and formed a circle. Dawn located Karin and gave her a little wave.

"She's gonna be tough," Carla said, noting the wave. "Hope you've got your best defensive shoes on."

"You bet." Dawn laughed and pointed to her legs. "I put on my new defensive legs, too, just in case." Karin would be a test for them, no doubt about it.

She just wished that Karin had stayed at North Park in the first place. At Sunday's forum, she'd gotten actively involved in the discussion. She'd also made friends with several of the kids, including Nathan and Troy, who had made a surprise appearance at Nathan's urging.

Dawn smiled inwardly about that. Now there were fourteen kids at the forum, and it looked like the group would continue to grow.

"Play defense the way you recruit kids for forum, and you're bound to win," Rev Steve had told her Sunday with a pat on the back.

Dawn closed her eyes tightly and said a little prayer for reassurance. She just hoped she could do her part to keep the Academy scoring down. Suddenly, she felt her stomach flip-flopping and wished the game would get started so she could quit being nervous.

"All right," Susan said, patting each girl on the back as they gathered on the North Park sideline. "Let's get fired up!"

"Remember," Alan cautioned, kneeling in the center of the circle and looking around from girl to girl, "keep moving on offense and be sure of your passes. Okay?" They all nodded. "If you feel tired, signal me, and we'll get somebody new on the field. And play defense—especially halfbacks and fullbacks! Don't give up on the ball and don't get pulled out of your zone." He looked around again. "Any last words from anyone?"

"Can we pray?" Dawn asked suddenly.

"Forget it," Wendy inserted. "You pray, I'll play."

"You can each say your own prayer if you want," Alan said quickly. "Take a few seconds." He closed his eyes and bowed his head, and Dawn joined him. She didn't look to see if anyone else was following their lead, but she hoped they were.

Alan stood. "Let's go get a victory." He held out his hand and they gathered around. "One-two-three, Polar power!" they shouted and then broke out onto the field to the cheers of their fans.

On the far side of the field, the Academy Chieftans were shouting their own words of encouragement. Then they, too, raced onto the field as the referee blew his whistle and looked to his linesmen to be sure they were prepared. Each waved a green card in his hand, signaling ready.

Dawn ran to the center of the field and gave each of the forwards a pat of encouragement.

"Good luck, Dawn." It was Karin.

"You, too," she replied, reaching out a hand to wish her former teammate well. Wendy scowled at the exchange as Dawn ran past to take her position.

The referee blew his whistle to get started, and one of Academy's center forwards kicked off. The game moved rapidly. Both offensive units moved the ball quickly up and down the field, but neither team could get a good open shot. Time and again, Dawn intercepted the ball, sometimes booting it long and hard back upfield, at other times distributing it to one of her wings.

The coaches substituted freely, but both Wendy and Dawn remained on the field the entire time. Wendy seemed lethargic and couldn't seem to get the North Park offense untracked. Meanwhile, the Academy offense started getting stronger. Dawn and her supporting fullbacks found themselves under serious attack.

Only Dawn's extra efforts kept two shots from going in, and with five minutes left, it appeared as if it was going to be a scoreless period. It was at that point that Academy made its first clean breakaway. Suddenly, Dawn found herself facing a two-on-one by Karin and one of her center-forward teammates. Dawn concentrated on Karin, figuring she would take the shot, but kept a wary eye on the other girl.

Karin made a quick pass to the forward, then got a return pass just as fast when Dawn turned to challenge the other girl. Dawn whirled around to help cut off what obviously was going to be a shot attempt, but her heel dropped into a small hole and she stumbled sideways.

"Dawn!" Beth shouted her name and took her eyes off Karin as Dawn fell. Reacting quickly, Karin pulled up and shot the ball hard to Beth's right into the near corner of the net. Academy was ahead, 1-0.

"You okay?" It was Karin who reached Dawn first, as

she disgustedly sat up on her knees.

"Yeah, I'm fine. Nice shot."

"Lucky," Karin replied. "Thanks for falling." She gave Dawn a sympathetic smile, and Dawn accepted an outstretched hand from her and stood up. Karin turned back upfield.

"Sorry," Beth said as she booted the ball back toward the referee and walked over to Dawn. "That was my fault. I shouldn't have looked away."

Dawn shook her head. "It was that stupid hole. It's pretty hard to keep your concentration when a team-mate goes flying in front of you. Let's tighten it up and shut 'em down the rest of the way."

The ball had barely gotten into play when Wendy broke out of her lackluster attitude and went to work—as if to show her arch-rival that she was not going to be outdone. Dribbling into the neutral zone at midfield, she chipped the ball across to Tricia, then sprinted in behind the left halfback and signaled for a lead pass back. Tricia complied, sending a nice ball between the defenders. Wendy collected it with her thigh.

As the ball dropped at her feet, the center midfielder charged over to tackle, but Wendy drew the ball back, changed directions and touched the ball into the open space where the halfback had been playing. She waved her right arm at Tricia as if directing her into a position to take another pass, then took the ball herself.

The center fullback set up to challenge, and Wendy drove straight at her as if she were going to run her down. Instead, she stepped over the ball, and—quickly changing directions—left the defender sprawling as she blasted a shot right past the keeper. Less than a minute had passed since Karin had scored, and now the score was 1-1.

Just before the half, Wendy went on the attack again, only this time it was her teammates who set her up for the score. Carla took a crossing ball from Dotty, penetrated deep along the left touchline, and then chipped a pass back over the right fullback.

Wendy hurtled in to control the pass and get the shot off, and the center fullback dived to try to knock the ball away. Instead, she tangled up Wendy with her feet and Wendy fell hard. The left linesman raised his flag to communicate with the referee, who blew his whistle and signaled a charging foul against the sweeperback.

Wendy leaped up grinning and waved to her father, who had moved into the area behind the goal with his camera. The referee placed the ball at the 12-yard maker in the box for a penalty kick, which Wendy promptly blasted past the goalie for the score. The half ended with the Polars up 2-1.

"That'll show her," Wendy said between clenched teeth as they huddled together near their bench.

"What? Who?" Susan asked.

"Nothing," the Polars' star striker responded. She walked away from the assistant coach, grabbed the water bottle and poured some on her head before taking a big drink. Susan shook her head as Wendy walked back to the sidelines and stared across the field at the Chieftans.

The first twenty minutes of the second half looked like a carbon copy of the opening period. Neither team could get an attack built up. Then, just as quickly as before, the fireworks began.

A penalty against Ginger set up the next Academy score, and the Chieftans covered the indirect free kick perfectly with Karin connecting on a high, hard shot that was virtually unstoppable.

Once more Wendy responded with a beautiful shot of her own. With ten minutes left, it was 3-2 Polars.

At the eight-minute mark, a new Academy front line came in and used their freshness to go on the attack, pressuring a weary Dawn and Jeannie into sagging back into a deep defense just in front of the goal.

As one of the center forwards tried to slip in for a wall pass from the wing, Dawn saw her chance to put the girl offside and stepped ahead to do so. But the referee didn't call it, and the forward took the pass and punched it home for the tying score.

"She was offside!" Dawn protested to the official. From the sidelines, Alan and Susan were yelling the same thing. The official, whistle clenched between his teeth, shook his head no and waved to the teams to get the play going again from midfield.

Alan kicked disgustedly at the ground as the Polars set up for their kickoff.

Wendy took the ball and charged upfield, but Karin cut her off and intercepted a long crossing pass to Allison, who was in at Carla's wing. Karin feinted to her left and then took off with the ball down the middle of the field. Wendy stayed with her, bumping her twice and then sprinting past her into the area between Dawn and Trini.

"Get out of the way!" she shouted at Trini. "I've got her."

Karin was just paces away, and Trini moved to the side as Wendy held her position, challenging the other team's star to run over her. Karin gritted her teeth, charged ahead, then made a brilliant back-footed pass to a teammate who was trailing close behind.

As her teammate took the ball, Karin crashed head-on into Wendy, and both girls fell into Dawn. The trio went down in a heap as the other Academy girl made a nice chip shot over Beth's outstretched hands to score.

Wendy, Karin, and Dawn were all getting up when Wendy suddenly turned and shoved Karin back down. Karin did a backward somersault, leaped up and charged Wendy, knocking her to the ground and falling on top of her. Both the referee and the linesman descended on the girls immediately. The coaches came running onto the field.

"Out! Get 'em both out of here!" the official shouted, jerking a thumb toward the sidelines. Taking out a small notepad, he wrote down their jersey numbers and signaled a red card to both benches.

Alan grabbed Wendy by the shoulders and half-pulled her toward the sidelines. "That was an idiotic thing to do."

Wendy didn't say anything. She jerked free from Alan's grasp and stormed over to the sideline, where she sat down on the bench.

"He's right. That was stupid," Dawn said to Beth as they watched the girls go. "Now we don't have her anymore this game and we lose her next game, too. It's an automatic one-game suspension for fighting."

"She shouldn't even have been down here on defense," Beth added.

The conclusion of the game was anticlimactic. When the final whistle blew, it was still 4-3 for Academy. The teams met at the center of the field to exchange handshakes, and then the Polars walked dejectedly back to their locker room.

"Hey, cheer up," Wendy said as they took off their sweaty uniforms. "We've lost before. We'll be back."

"What're you so happy about?" Carla grumbled. "You have to sit out next game, too."

"Yeah, well, big deal. I put that has-been in her place. She can't play next game either, so I'll keep my lead."

"Is that all you think about?" Ginger snapped.

"Yeah, it is," Wendy replied coolly. "I'm going to win that trophy. And even if we lose the first couple of games, we'll get a lot of wins when I get back. So you better think about my scoring, too." She swept up her gym bag and marched out of the locker room as the rest of the team stared in disbelief at the door.

Just as the team feared, they couldn't generate an offense in the next outing either. The game ended 1-0 for
the Brownsville Orioles, and only a penalty kick from a
questionable tripping foul set up the Oriole score. A
positive factor was the new diamond defense, which
Dawn and her teammates worked to near perfection. At
times, in fact, it seemed as if no matter where the Oriole
forwards turned to pass, there was a Polar in line to pick
it off.

As the North Park team trudged off the field at the
game's conclusion, Dawn sensed a mood of optimism in
her teammates despite the defeat.

"We played that new defense pretty darn good,
didn't we?" she said to Susan as they walked back
toward the gym.

"You bet," she answered. "I think it's going to be
tougher and tougher for the opposition to get the ball
into our nets."

"Dawn Davis and the diamond defense!" exclaimed
Beth. "From here on out, no one beats the Double D!
Right?"

"Right," Dawn laughed. "But it takes all of us to
make that thing work, you know."

"Sure, but we've been building around you," Beth
responded, putting an arm around Dawn's shoulders.
"You've been making some super stops out there. Sure
makes my job a lot easier."

"If we get scoring again," Alan said, "there's no
doubt we're going to start winning. It was a fluke that
Brownsville got that penalty shot on us today. You guys
keep playing tough D, and it's going to take a really
great shooter to beat us."

Like Karin, Dawn thought. But there was no sense in
worrying about her now. It would be weeks before the

Polars had to take on Academy again. Maybe by that time, she'd even figure out how to stop somebody as good as Karin.

Dawn wiped the perspiration from her brow and flopped down on the grass in front of the makeshift goal. Rev Steve poured a cup of water from the thermos and passed it to her.

"Good workout," he said. "At least from my view."

"Yeah," she gasped. "You weren't kidding when you said you were going to make it tougher and tougher. I just can't stop some of those shots."

He nodded. "I know. But I'm bigger and stronger and I've got too much experience. What you really need is to work against someone your own age, size, and speed. That way I could get a better feel for what you're doing right and wrong."

"You've convinced me. Any candidates?"

He peered at his watch and glanced over to the parking lot as if expecting someone. Almost as if on cue, a tall, slender girl with strawberry blond hair came wheeling into the lot on her bike. Karin.

Dawn stared, and then looked back to Rev Steve.

"Are you serious?" she inquired.

"Dead serious. You said you want to work against someone, so why not go against someone really good? Besides, you two are friends, aren't you?"

"Well, yeah, but . . ."

"But nothing," he replied. "It'll do you both some good. She needs to keep working on her shooting, and you need to work on defense." He stopped talking and looked up as Karin walked up to them. "Hi, Karin." He greeted her with a warm smile.

Dawn swallowed hard and got to her feet. "Hi," she said, suddenly self-conscious. "Rev Steve says maybe we should work out together. What do you think?"

Karin shrugged. "Sure, I guess. At least for today."

"Yeah. For today. Okay?" Both girls nodded, as if reassuring themselves that there was nothing wrong with practicing with a member of an arch-rival team.

"Glad to hear it," Rev Steve boomed. "Let's quit standing around and get to work."

The next hour raced past as Rev Steve put them through their paces. When the time was up, he smiled broadly and tossed the water jug their way.

"Well, what do you think?" he said. "Worth it?"

"No doubt," Dawn responded. "I think I learned more this hour than I have since the season started."

Karin nodded in agreement. "Me, too." She turned to Dawn. "You know, you're really getting strong at that position. It does me a lot of good to try to work against someone as good as you."

Dawn felt a warm glow at the praise. "Thanks; I feel the same. I know when I stop your shots, I'm stopping the best."

"Now that this mutual admiration society has been formed, can we decide whether to keep it going?" Rev Steve interrupted.

The girls laughed.

"How about if we do a couple more sessions together, and then you can each go on your merry way and finish out the season. I know I can be a lot more help if I don't have to be out there booting the ball around."

The girls glanced at each other and nodded.

"Okay, partner," Dawn said, holding out a hand, which Karin shook. "Deal?"

"Deal. Just don't tell my teammates."

"Mine either, especially Wendy. She'd be screaming from here to Canada and back if she ever found out about this." And despite the laugh she shared with the others, inside she thought, *And that's the truth.*

9
Discovering Wendy

"So, you turkeys are already 0-2. I thought this was going to be your year to go undefeated!" Troy leaned back and chuckled.

"Gee, I'm really pleased you decided to join us here today," Dawn replied calmly. "I can't think of anyone else I'd rather see . . . except maybe Godzilla or King Kong or the Blob."

Nathan and Karin erupted into laughter, and Dawn just smiled sweetly at Troy. The rest of the class had already exited, but the four friends had remained to talk for a few minutes.

"We wouldn't have lost, if Wendy hadn't gotten so intent on stopping Karin here," Dawn went on. "Wendy got tossed and then we lost." She stopped. "Hey, that rhymes."

"I got tossed, too, you know," Karin said indignantly.

"Yeah, but thanks to your pass, your team scored on the play. We definitely needed Wendy—we just don't have anyone else who can score."

"Maybe next year Karin will be back," Troy said quickly, glancing sideways at her as he spoke. "I know I'd like to see her come to North Park High."

Karin smiled prettily. "Guess it all depends on how the rest of this year goes."

"In other words, if we can get Wendy's attitude adjusted," Nathan interjected. "You know, I can remember when she was really nice. We used to be neighbors, and I liked her."

"Maybe we should pray for her," Karin said softly, glancing around. The others grew quiet.

Finally Troy nodded. "Couldn't hurt," he said.

"I'll pray," Karin said. "After all, I'm the one with the most to gain if she changes."

"We'd all gain if she changed," Dawn said. She bowed her head, and the others followed suit. It seemed like minutes passed before Karin's quiet voice broke the silence.

"Lord," she began. "I'm not real great at praying, but I've got a favor to ask. There's a girl in our town named Wendy, and she needs Your help." She stopped, and Dawn, Nathan, and Troy remained silent. Only their breathing interrupted the calm. "I'd like for Wendy to change and become a nicer person, Lord. I think maybe she's got a lot of pressure on her, and that's what makes her act mean. But, Lord, I hope you'll help her to change." She stopped again.

Dawn thought she was finished and started to raise her head, but Karin still had her head bowed and eyes closed tight.

"And, Lord, help me be a more understanding person, too, so that I don't always get so upset with her or . . . or with anyone else, either. Amen."

They all looked up and Karin shrugged. "Well, things can't be any worse, and maybe they'll get better. Who knows?"

They all laughed and stood to leave.

"You've just got to come back to North Park next year," Dawn implored, as they started toward the stairway. "We really want you here." Nathan and Troy nodded.

"Besides," Dawn added, as she skipped ahead on the stairs, "I want you scoring goals for *our* team and not dumb old Academy's."

"That's a great Christian attitude!" Nathan called after her. He caught up with Dawn and walked along with her and her parents to their car. "Troy and I are coming to watch you guys play Valley."

"Great! We're going to start our winning streak with that one. Our defense is going to shut them down."

"Good." He took her hand and squeezed it. "It won't hurt you to have Wendy back scoring some points, either, you know."

"I know," she said half-heartedly. "Too bad we don't have Karin, too. I really do like her."

"Me, too. We'll just keep working on her; that's all there is to it."

"And Wendy, too, I guess," Dawn added glumly, "although that's probably a lost cause." She hung her head for a couple seconds, and then brightened. "Thanks for being part of the forum, Nathan. I think it's really going great."

"Me, too," he said. Then he turned and gave Dawn's parents a wave. "I've got to run. Bye, everyone."

"Nice young man," Dawn's mother said, watching him go.

"Yeah," she answered, still feeling blue about Karin and Wendy.

"You don't sound so sure," Dad noted.

"Oh, I'm not down about Nathan," Dawn assured him. "We were just talking about Wendy. It doesn't seem fair that she should act the way she does—and drive someone else away because of it."

"Maybe she really doesn't want to act mean," Mom said. "Maybe it's just a big front."

"Huh?" Dawn looked blank.

"Maybe she's just afraid to be nice because she thinks it'll keep her from being a good, tough soccer player. Didn't you say she seemed to be driven to win some trophy or something?"

"The league scoring trophy. Her dad's sponsoring it with his newspaper, and she really wants to win."

"So that she can look important to her father?"

Dawn stopped in her tracks and turned to face her parents. "Do you think that's it?" she said. She turned back around before they could answer, talking to herself. "That's *got* to be it. Her dad's so hyped up about her being a star player, that she's got to prove to him that she is. I wonder if I could talk to her. . . ."

"Dawn."

"Just a minute, Dad, I've got to think about something."

"*Dawn.*"

"Dad, what? I told you—" She stopped and looked back. Her mother and father were standing together beside their car, waiting with the door ajar. "Oh," she said, blushing. She hurried back and scrambled inside as her parents joined her in a laugh.

She plotted the rest of the afternoon how to best approach Wendy, and finally decided to start with Tricia. "After all," she said aloud to herself in the mirror, "Tricia *is* Wendy's only known friend."

Dawn slept fitfully and hurried to get dressed and off to school. She wanted to be waiting at the corner by The Huddle when Tricia walked by on her way to school. Dawn sat on the step outside, trying to look as if she just naturally happened to be there. After a few minutes, she started reading her English assignment and became so absorbed in the story that she didn't hear the sound of approaching footsteps.

"What are you doing here?" asked a voice.

"Tricia! You surprised me!" Dawn gasped, jerking back.

"Sorry." Tricia smiled. "Are you lost?"

"No, I was just going to school and realized I'd be plenty early, so I stopped to read for a few minutes."

Tricia gave her an odd stare. "Dawn, this is three blocks out of your way."

Dawn gave her a sheepish grin. "I'm not a very good liar, am I? Actually, I was waiting here for you."

"How come?"

"I need to ask you some questions . . . about Wendy. I figured if I caught you here, we could talk without anyone interrupting."

"Or listening in?"

"Something like that."

"So, talk already," Tricia said, as they started up the street. "If you went this much out of your way, it must be important."

"It is," Dawn said. "Do you think Wendy's changed a lot lately? You know, the last few months, or the last year or so?"

"Why are you asking me?"

"Because you guys are friends, that's why. Aren't you?"

"Sort of," Tricia replied after a slight pause. "We were, anyway. She's been pretty hard to talk to lately. I'd drop her, but every time I think about doing that, I feel guilty. You know what I mean?"

Dawn nodded. "What's bothering her, anyway?"

"I don't know. Maybe it's her dad. He's always pushing her so hard on this soccer thing. She wants to make him proud of her, but sometimes I think she'd like to chuck it all and just quit completely. He'd probably freak if she did."

Dawn breathed a long, slow sigh. Before she could

90

respond, Tricia spoke again.

"She knows she's got a lot of enemies now, but she just doesn't know how to change her act. At least, that's the feeling I get. Like I said, we're not as close as we used to be."

They walked on in silence for a few yards before Dawn spoke again.

"Maybe she just needs to know she doesn't have to act so stuck up and mean to succeed. I'm going to try to talk to her. Don't tell her we talked, okay?"

Tricia nodded.

"I may not get anywhere, but at least I can let her know that some of her teammates would be willing to go halfway toward making peace if she wants to try." The girls had reached the school grounds and paused to go different ways. "See you at lunch. You ready to beat Valley?"

"You bet. Tonight we break into the win column."

Maybe with Wendy, too, Dawn thought as she watched Tricia hurry away. At least she'd put a notch in the "try" column.

"Right after the game—win, lose, or draw," Dawn muttered to herself. She tightened her shoelaces and stamped her feet on the floor to make sure her shoes were snug.

"What's right after the game?" Carla asked, pulling her jersey into place.

"Just talking to myself," Dawn answered. "You ready? I feel like we're going to win."

"I *know* we're going to win," Carla said. "Especially with you-know-who back in the pack." She jerked a thumb toward Wendy's locker. "I'm going out to start warming up. Come on."

"Be there in a minute," Dawn said, looking back toward Wendy. "You go ahead."

Carla looked at Dawn questioningly, then shrugged. "Suit yourself," she said, heading out the door.

Dawn fiddled absently with a shoelace while trying to muster the courage to say something.

Wendy, sitting on the floor and stretching her right leg, seemed oblivious to Dawn's presence. Then she stood, touched her toes, and gave a little gasp. She sat back on the bench and rubbed her right ankle.

"You okay?" Dawn asked.

"I'll be all right. My ankle's been bothering me the last few days." She gave a half-hearted wave.

Dawn started to leave, then stopped. "I've been meaning to ask you something."

Wendy looked up with an annoyed expression. "What's up?"

"Well," Dawn began. "Well, uh, you know when I'm in position to make the stop, I want to get the ball out of there as quick as possible. But, I'm not real sure where I should try to distribute the ball." She paused again. "What I'm saying is, where would the forwards want the ball?"

"I'm glad you asked that," Wendy said, brightening. "I was going to say something about that, anyway. If you'd try to get the kick out wide, it would set us up better to take off with the ball. When it comes down the middle, if the halfbacks aren't in good position, the other team just gets the ball right back." She had turned to face Dawn now and was animated in her explanation, drawing a diagram in the air as she spoke.

Dawn returned Wendy's smile. "Thanks. I appreciate the advice."

"No problem. If I can help anymore, just let me know."

Dawn gritted her teeth and nodded. She started for the door again, but once more stopped and looked back. "Maybe you and I can get together some time after practice and work on a few shots?"

Wendy seemed pleasantly surprised at the invitation. She stood up, flinching slightly as she put pressure on her ankle, and walked over to join Dawn at the door. "Yeah," she said. "Maybe we can."

They walked out together. Now it was Dawn's turn to flinch as she saw Carla standing twenty feet away with a big question mark all over her face.

Wendy held out her hand to Dawn. "Have a good game," she said. She turned and jogged over toward the coaches.

Carla stared in Dawn's direction, and Dawn hurried over to her friend's side.

"What was *that* all about?"

"Nothing. She told me to have a good game."

"You working on becoming her second known friend or something?"

"Come off it," Dawn snapped. "She just looked a little down, so I figured she could use a few words of support. After all, she does play well, you know."

"Yeah, I know," Carla responded. "In case you haven't noticed, she always lets me know. And she never has a word or two of support for her good old buddy, Tank." She walked away.

Dawn hurried to catch up. "Look, Carla, I'm sorry. I didn't mean to upset you. I was thinking maybe we could get Wendy to change her attitude a little if we made a few attempts to be friendlier. Okay?"

Carla shrugged and kept walking.

"Maybe you should try it, too," Dawn persisted, keeping pace with her as they jogged onto the field. "She might just change, you know?"

"Look," Carla said, turning angrily. "*You* be Miss Goody-goody with her all you want, but keep me out of it. I don't like her, and it doesn't take anybody real brilliant to see she doesn't like me, either. If you want to be her friend instead of mine, fine!"

"Hey, I never said—" Dawn began, but Carla pulled away and ran off. At that precise moment, Wendy jogged past and gave Dawn a wave.

Oh, brilliant! Dawn exclaimed to herself. *What's going on, anyway? Hey, God—can't I help Wendy without losing Carla in the process? What good does it do to be nice to someone you don't like if it means losing someone you do?*

The Polars won big over the Valley Springs Raiders. Not only did Wendy play her usual great offensive game, but Carla played as if possessed, scoring one goal and making two great passes to Wendy to set up two more.

But when Dawn went over to congratulate Carla afterward, her friend just turned away and left. By the time Dawn got home for supper, she felt as though she'd been hit by another soccer ball. She picked at her food and then asked to be excused to go to her room. She was sitting silently on her bed when there was a knock on the door.

"Come in."

"You want to talk about it, or shall I leave you alone?" asked Dad.

Dawn shook her head. "It's okay. But I don't know if there's anything to talk about." She explained what had happened at the game. "I really blew it, huh? Wendy will be the same old snob she's always been, and now I don't have Carla anymore, either."

Tears ran down Dawn's face, and her father held out a Kleenex. Dawn wiped off her face and blew her nose.

"I think you did the right thing," Dad said, sitting down at the end of Dawn's bed. "Sounds to me like Wendy's got a king-sized chip on her shoulder. The only decent thing to do is just what you tried. And you did

94

say she acted friendlier, didn't you?"

Dawn nodded, snuffling. "But I didn't think it would hurt Carla so much, you know? Now what do I do? If I back off on Wendy, she'll probably act worse than ever. But if I keep trying to be friendly to her, then Carla won't talk to me."

"If I know Carla," said Dad, "she's probably sitting on her bed right now feeling just as miserable as you. Why don't you give her a call?"

Dawn gave her dad a hug, which was interrupted by the telephone. She ran to answer it.

"It's Carla!" she mouthed to her father, who had followed her out to the hallway.

"Oh. You did? You are? That's exactly what I've been doing. Look, I'm really sorry—No, you don't have to apologize." She laughed aloud. "Okay. We were both jerks. Now we can be jerky friends. Again." She sighed and leaned back against the wall, the phone cradled against her ear and a big grin on her face.

Her father grinned and headed downstairs.

10
No Slack Time

With Dawn leading the defense and Wendy back at full stride alongside a suddenly aggressive Carla, the Polars chalked up four successive wins. At the same time, Dawn worked harder at bringing Wendy out of her shell, even staying two nights after practice on the pretense of needing extra help.

Carla understood what Dawn was up to, but she gave a vehement no to Dawn's invitations to help. She wished Dawn well in her "missionary work," as she called it, but she wasn't going to participate.

On Saturdays, Dawn continued her workouts with Karin and Rev Steve. She found that she was not only getting better at soccer, but she and Karin were becoming very good friends. The friendship was fed by their times together at the youth forum, too, where their special project was well underway.

The kids were gathering non-perishable food to send to a sister congregation in Chicago, which was helping stock food banks for the upcoming winter months.

They had also begun a letter-writing campaign to members of Congress to help release the more than two billion pounds of government surplus food sitting in storage—a revelation from Rev Steve that had astounded the ever-growing group of teens. Nearly half of the ninth through twelfth grade youth had joined the group, much to Dawn's and Rev Steve's delight. Dawn was feeling good about life in general, even though her progress with Wendy was still in a "wait and see" pattern.

After practice one Thursday, Dawn stopped on the grass outside the gym to clean off her shoes. Wendy walked over, newspaper in hand.

"We're 4-2 now. One of these days Academy is going to slip again, too, I'll bet," Wendy noted. She pointed to a story in the paper about the junior soccer league standings. Alongside the article, prominently pictured for the second time in the season, was a photo of Wendy about to knock in her eighteenth goal. The caption read: "Polar Star Still Leading in Race for Trophy."

"Nice picture," Dawn said. "How far ahead are you?"

"Just two goals," Wendy answered, her countenance darkening. "Karin's got sixteen. Academy may be the Polars' arch-rivals, but she's mine!"

Dawn swallowed, wondering what Wendy would say if she knew what good friends she and Karin had become. "Well," she said lightly, "she's making you work harder. Right?"

"Sure. But I could probably be up by two or three more if Carla wasn't always hogging the ball. How come she's so fired up about scoring all of a sudden? Dumb Tank."

Dawn set her jaw and reached over and took the paper away from her teammate. "You know," she said, as Wendy looked up in surprise, "you're not a half bad person, but if you keep saying nasty things about people, you're never going to have any friends."

Wendy frowned. "Huh? You mean me calling Carla

tank?" she scoffed. "Come on. It's just something I do."

"Well, you shouldn't," Dawn said firmly. "Besides, Carla's done more than her share of making decent passes to you to set up goals. If you'd lighten up a little, maybe the rest of the team wouldn't mind being friends with you." Suddenly Dawn cut herself off, surprised at her own daring.

Wendy just sat there, looking grim. Dawn glanced over the top of the ball at her before speaking again.

"I'm sorry, Wendy, but I had to say it. If you'd be a little nicer to the others, they'd be nicer, too." Still Wendy said nothing, so Dawn shrugged and turned away.

"See ya later," Wendy said softly.

Dawn stopped in her tracks and looked back over her shoulder. "Yeah. See you later."

She hurried off to the locker room and was chatting with Carla when Wendy shuffled in and walked silently past them.

Carla grimaced and stood. "I gotta take off. I'm dead tired from practice and I've got a ton of homework. You'd think Coach, at least, would ease off on us. I've got more to do in his class than any other."

"That's the truth," Dawn agreed. "Maybe it's his way of telling us we aren't good enough for the team. We can't play if we're flunking, right?" The girls both laughed.

"I, uh, I hope you do okay. With the class, I mean."

Wendy's quiet voice stopped Carla as if she'd been hit with a board. "Wh-what?" she stammered.

"I said," Wendy repeated, shifting around on the bench, "I hope you do okay with your classes, because we need you on the team. Okay?"

Carla looked uneasily at Dawn. "Well, thanks. I appreciate that." She swallowed hard. "Well, I really do have to get going. See you in the morning." She gave

Dawn a little wave and turned toward Wendy. "You, too, Wendy."

Wendy smiled ever so slightly, gave a little wave, and turned her back to the girls.

Carla raised her eyebrows, her eyes wide in disbelief. Dawn just grinned and shrugged.

"You think she's for real, or is it just an act to keep me making good passes?" Carla asked breathlessly as they hurried down the hall to English class. "Did you tell her I was mad and wouldn't pass the ball to her anymore?"

"I think she's really trying to change," Dawn said.

"Maybe. Seems a little fishy to me."

"Well, wait and see," Dawn answered. "What've you got to lose?"

"It's almost too much of a shock for me to handle. The next thing you know, we're going to walk into English class and Mrs. Kuhlman's going to tell me I have a straight A average."

"Look," Dawn said, as they reached the classroom door, "with Wendy, we're talking major change. But if you were getting an A in English, that would rank in the category of miracles." She dodged out of Carla's reach as the bell rang, and both girls earned a frown from the teacher as they scrambled, laughing, into their seats.

The victory over Roseville's Rockets that afternoon was almost anticlimactic, compared with the way Wendy acted toward her teammates. Each time she scored, she circled both the forward and halfback lines, slapping hands with the other girls and giving the high sign to Dawn and the other fullbacks. On one occasion she had a sure goal, but passed to Carla instead to give her an easy point. When the game was over—a 6-1 North Park win—Wendy even hugged a couple of her team-

99

mates before running over to her wildly cheering parents.

It was just a taste of things to come.

Over the next two weeks, as the team practiced and played its way into October, nasty, self-centered Wendy suddenly became everybody's friend. At first the other girls were cautious. But by the second week they were starting to cheer for Wendy when she made a good play—something only Tricia had been doing before.

After a second win over Edgemont, Wendy was laughing and cheering with her teammates, exchanging "high fives" and accepting congratulations. When she came to Dawn, she stopped and gave her a hug.

"Thanks," she said softly. "I appreciate what you did for me."

"Was that Wendy?" her mother said. She had come up to congratulate Dawn as the other girl loped off the field.

"Yeah," Dawn replied, watching her with a warm feeling. "She's changed so much. I think we could even turn out to be friends."

"I'm glad," Mom answered.

"Me, too."

Carla still remained skeptical, and Dawn noticed that Wendy treated Carla with a little more distance than she did the rest of the team.

"I still get the feeling that she's waiting to do or say something nasty to me," Carla explained. "All of a sudden she's too good to be true. It makes me uneasy, that's all."

They were walking into the church as they talked, and Dawn agreed that it did seem too good to be true.

"Tell me again what you said to her," Carla urged.

"I just told her that if she'd try to be friendly once in a while, maybe everyone else would be friendly to her, too. Really! That's all I said. Suddenly, she's Miss Nice."

"Well, Miss Nice or not, I'm going to be careful," Carla said.

Troy and Nathan were sitting directly in front of them. Just after the bell, Karin hurried in and settled into the seat next to Troy, who smiled happily at her arrival.

"Oh, brother," whispered Carla, giving Dawn a poke in the ribs. "Another love story. Soon I won't have any unattached friends left."

Rev Steve wheeled a portable blackboard to the front of the group and greeted them. In his soft, gentle voice, he opened the forum with prayer.

"Dear God, thank You for bringing us together here in our warm, safe church so that we might help our fellow human beings who do not share our comforts. Inspire in us the love and determination to serve those who are in need. And even though we are a small group, show us how we can work to change the world and end its hunger. Amen."

"Amen," they echoed, looking up.

"Well, I've got good news and bad news. Which do you want to hear first?"

"The good," Nathan said. "Unless the bad is really bad?"

The class members laughed, and Rev Steve shook his head. "No, not really bad. But not really good, either. Okay, I'll start with the good. As of yesterday, we had this many pounds of food gathered in our little warehouse downtown." On the blackboard, he wrote 3,800. The kids erupted into cheers. "I agree," he said. "Pretty good for just four weeks. We should easily surpass our goal of 6,000 pounds by the end of October."

He paced in front of the blackboard before continuing.

"The bad news is that I received this letter from our

sister congregation in Chicago. They've had a setback with their transportation arrangements, and they're asking us to make our own arrangements for shipping the food from here to there."

"How are we supposed to do that?" asked Carla.

"Yeah," Bob Young inserted, peering over the top of his thick glasses. "We don't have a truck to haul 6,000 pounds of food. That'd cost a bundle."

"You're right," the minister said grimly. "How does $2,800 grab you?"

The kids moaned. "I don't know how we'll get that kind of money in just a few weeks," Rev Steve said. "But are you willing to give it a try?"

The kids nodded assent.

"Good. Now we've got a new challenge. Any ideas?"

"We could ask our parents," Monica commented. "If every kid got a hundred dollars or so, we'd have enough."

Some of the others shifted uneasily at the suggestion.

"Our forum group pledged to do this project as a way to show what *we* can do," Dawn declared, "not to see what we can get from our parents. If we go to them now, we're just copping out."

A murmur of agreement rippled through the room.

By the end of the session, several ideas—ranging from a community car wash to a bake sale to sponsoring a concert—had been written on the blackboard.

"I like that last idea, especially if we could get the college to donate the space," Rev Steve mused.

Dawn and Carla exchanged glances, and Dawn raised her hand.

"Our assistant soccer coach is at the college," she said. "Susan LaFollette. Maybe Carla and I can talk with her about it."

"Oh, yes. The one I met when you got bashed with the soccer ball" Rev Steve said with a grin.

102

Both Dawn and Nathan blushed at mention of the incident.

"I say go for it!" Rev Steve boomed. "We'll use anything we can to our advantage."

The bell rang, and the kids started out. Nathan pulled out the chair he'd been sitting on and slipped into the row beside Dawn.

"Seems like we haven't had many chances to see each other lately," he began.

"I know," she said wistfully. "It's been so busy at school, and our practices have been going long. Coach says he'll cut back if we have good games this week. I see you guys are still winning."

"Yeah, so far. Any chance you can make it to our Friday game? We're playing against Academy."

"If we win Thursday, we might have Friday off. Then I could come for sure. I feel bad that I haven't been able to watch you play."

He shrugged. "It's okay. Next year it'll be a lot easier, when we're all over at the high school together."

Karin and Troy came over to join them.

"Karin doesn't have practice Friday, so she's coming to our game," said Troy. "You gonna make it, Dawn?"

"Maybe. Alan hasn't canceled our practice. Of course, we're not in first place like some other teams I know." She gave Karin a good-natured shove.

"Well, we were thinking maybe the four of us could go out for pizza afterward. What do you think?"

Dawn brightened. "I think it sounds great. But, as I said, it depends on my old slavedriver coach. He said if we have good games this week, he might cut back on our practices."

"As much as I hate to encourage the opposition, I hope you win both games big," Karin said with a laugh. "My mother's not real excited about my dating yet, but if I was going along with you—" she reached out and tapped Dawn—"I know it would be okay. So, come on Polars. Go, fight, win!"

"You going to cheer for us like that, when we're playing Academy Friday?" Troy teased.

"Well," she hedged. "Until I officially become a Polar again next year, I'd better cheer for my own school. But I promise to mutter under my breath, *Yea, Troy! Yea, Nathan!* every time you do something good."

"If I can come Friday, I'll call you Thursday night. Okay?" Dawn gave Nathan's hand a squeeze and headed up the stairs.

11
Double Date

Dawn booted the ball hard and watched with satisfaction as it sailed nearly to midfield. She eyed the rest of the balls in a line, took two steps back, and stepped into the next one, again hitting it long and hard.

The *thwack* of her soccer shoe as it struck the leather side of the ball was solid. Again she stopped to watch the flight of the soaring ball.

"Looking good." It was Susan, her ever-present clipboard in hand, walking up from behind the net.

Dawn beamed. "I think my clearing shots have really improved. When I get time to set them up, of course."

"Your whole game is looking sharp," Susan answered. "Seems like a long time ago that I asked you to boot one back to me on the practice field by the high school."

"Yeah," Dawn said with a little smile. "Just think— only three more games and the season will be over. How do you think we'll do?"

"We should beat Valley again with no problem. But Brownsville'll be tough, and then we've still got to take care of Academy. Brownsville only has two losses—just like us. And Academy is 10-1."

"We would've beat Brownsville the first time if we had been playing like we are now," Dawn argued. "I don't think they're as good as we are. But Academy . . . It sounds like they're getting better and better. And today's paper said Karin is even with Wendy in scoring. I sure wish she had stuck it out here, especially since Wendy's changed so much."

"Well, maybe Wendy wouldn't have been so quick to change with Karin around, you know?" Susan smiled. "It's easy to be friends when no one's trying to steal your thunder."

Dawn nodded glumly. She had been thinking that Wendy's change in attitude would make it easier for Karin to come back as a tenth-grader. But now, digesting Susan's words, she realized that Wendy was being very friendly with everyone except Carla—the only other team member who was scoring goals.

"I've got to move on," Susan noted. "What was it you wanted to ask me, anyway?"

"Huh?"

"When we were coming out for practice, you said you and Carla wanted to ask me something."

"Oh, yeah," Dawn said nervously. "We need your help—up at the college. I-I mean, if you can."

"What's it all about?"

Dawn explained about the youth forum and the money-raising project. "We were hoping that the college could have some sort of concert as a fund raiser for the group. All the money would go toward transportation costs for the food. What do you think?"

"I think it's great!" Susan exclaimed. "But I don't have any control over the college concerts. I'll be glad to run it past the dean's office tomorrow. In fact, the group I play with is having a concert this Saturday. Maybe we could be the ones to help."

"You play with a group?" Dawn said excitedly. "I didn't know that! What are you called?"

"The chamber orchestra."

"The chamber orchestra?" Dawn echoed in a low voice.

Susan laughed. "Exactly the reaction most people have, which is probably why we never get an audience. But, hey, we're pretty good. And if everyone in the community knew it was a benefit concert to help your youth group, I'll bet we'd draw a big crowd."

Dawn slowly nodded. "Sure. You could tell your dean that the kids would help get a big crowd if we could use it as a fund raiser."

Susan thought for a moment. "It would be a great way for the college to show the community that it's willing to help out a local group." She put an arm around Dawn's shoulder. "Can you get out of school tomorrow—middle of the day?"

"Maybe."

"This idea will work, but it has to get past the dean first. If you come along to help, I think he might give us the okay."

"Could I bring Carla along, too?"

"Why not?" Susan laughed. "We'll overwhelm him with numbers." She eyed the next soccer ball in the row and booted it upfield.

"Sure hope your music is better than your soccer," Dawn remarked as the ball fell back to the ground after flying only about twenty yards. "Of course," she added with a twinkle in her eye, "you are getting to be a pretty old lady."

"What!" Susan exclaimed, reaching for the next soccer ball as Dawn started to back away. "I'll show you who's an old lady!" Shrieking, Dawn raced away with Susan hot on her heels, as the other players stopped to stare in amazement.

"Don't look so sour," Susan admonished them as they left the dean's office the next day. "You got him to support your cause."

"Yeah, but with no admission fee," griped Carla. "How are we supposed to make any money with no admission fee?"

"Easy," Susan said. "Take up a collection. A free will offering."

"How do we do that?" Dawn responded.

"You've got twenty-five or thirty kids, don't you? Have some at each door to tell people about your cause and ask for their support. You might make a bundle."

"Might not make anything, either," Carla grumbled. "You think anyone wants to come hear a chamber orchestra?"

"Oh, you might find a person or two," Susan chuckled. "But you better get your youth group together right away and figure out how to advertise this thing. The auditorium holds about six hundred people, but we usually only get one or two hundred."

The girls had trouble keeping their minds on practice that afternoon. Finally they asked Alan if they could leave early to continue their planning, and he grudgingly agreed. It was Wednesday night anyway, and practice would be cut short for youth group release time.

By seven o'clock, nearly thirty kids were gathered in the forum meeting room, and Dawn and Carla had relayed their news.

"But what if nobody comes? Or what if they don't donate anything in the offering?" Nathan lamented.

Dawn shrugged. "Then I guess we put in a lot of effort for nothing. But if they do, we could end up with hundreds of dollars—maybe even a thousand dollars."

Everyone started talking excitedly, till Rev Steve interrupted by clapping his hands. He cleared his throat and spoke in his calm, clear voice. "I think we should go into this thing thinking that maybe—*maybe*—we can get an average of a dollar per person. So what we need to work on is getting that concert hall as full as possible. Aim for six hundred dollars. That's an important chunk of money."

Troy stood up. "I think we need to make posters to put all over town—in the schools, everywhere."

"Good idea," the minister said. "And someone needs to get the information together and get it over to the radio station. Maybe they'll broadcast it for us the next couple of days. Any volunteers?" Monica and Bob raised their hands at the same time, so he said quickly, "Great. A committee of two."

By evening's end, when they closed with a prayer, the group left determined to fill the concert hall no matter what—even if they had to personally invite every friend and relative to the event.

The game against Valley went as Susan had predicted. By midway through the second period, it was obvious that it would be a comfortable win. But the loudest cheers came when Alan gathered the team around him after the game and announced that they would have Friday off to be fully rested for the final week of play.

"It'll be a big week," he cautioned, "but if you girls play up to your capabilities, we should beat Brownsville on Tuesday. Then we'll have three good days to get ready for—" he paused for effect.

"Academy!" the girls all shouted. "Beat Academy!"

"All right!" he shouted in return. "Great game, Polars! See you all Monday."

That evening, Dawn got her folks' permission for the pizza date with Nathan. Then she gave him a call. "I'm coming to your game!" she began, barely giving him time to say hello. "Our practice is off for tomorrow."

"Terrific!" he exclaimed. "Did you call Karin yet?"

"No, but she'll be happy, too. Now we can go out for pizza and do a little more planning for the concert. Do you think anyone will come?"

"I sure hope so. I've been talking it up at the high school. Are your parents going?"

"They'd better!" Dawn answered. "How about yours?"

"They already had other plans. I'm a little worried that the same thing will happen with a lot of other people. It is kind of late notice."

"I know. Are you going by yourself, then?"

"Yeah."

"Why not go with us? My parents would be happy to have you come along, and so would I."

"That would be great! You sure?"

"Yes," she said, trying to emphasize just how sure she was.

"Good. I'll see you tomorrow. Win or lose, it'll be a good afternoon with you there." He laughed his usual warm, cheery laugh. "Oh, I've got one more question. Do you know anything about chamber music?"

"Not a thing. How about you?"

"Zilch," he chuckled. "I'm glad we'll be there together so I won't do something dumb—like applauding at the wrong spot or falling asleep."

"I'll poke you in the ribs if you do."

They said their goodbyes, and then Dawn got ready for bed. She had a restless night, alternating between dreams about holding hands with Nathan, getting smashed in the face by a soccer ball, and falling asleep in the concert hall with Nathan and her parents shaking her and shouting at her.

By the time she got to school next morning, she was already worn out. The day dragged by. Even in Alan's class, she found herself nodding off a couple of times.

But when the final bell rang, Dawn forgot her lack of sleep. She raced to grab her book bag, find Carla, and rush excitedly to the high school game. Twice Nathan caught her eye, and once he even gave her a little wave as he jogged to his position. Dawn blushed, thinking everyone in the stands must've noticed. After looking around, she realized—with just a touch of disappointment—that no one had.

Late in the game, the score was knotted at two. A halfback pass to Nathan was right on the mark, and he started into the middle with the ball. Jeff Baintree, a senior forward, looped across on Nathan's left to help, and Nathan lofted a kick in his direction.

As the ball made its downward arc, the defensive fullback jumped forward to head the ball back upfield and out of Jeff's path. But when the ball hit his head, it caromed off to the side—right back to Nathan, who feinted as if he were going to attempt a shot.

The fullback swerved to slide tackle Nathan, and the goalie dived desperately into Nathan's shooting line. Nathan spun away, screening both the fullback and the goalkeeper from the ball, and chipped a pass up and over the fullback to the waiting Baintree, who had nothing but open space in front of him.

With the fullback scrambling to get back, and the goalkeeper lying helplessly on his side, Baintree booted a hard, low shot into the right corner of the net.

North Park held off a final, desperate Academy attack. They had cleared the ball past midfield and were back on attack themselves when time ran out. The players and fans mobbed their goalie, Baintree, and Nathan before the players returned to center field to exchange handshakes with the disconsolate Academy squad.

As Nathan and Troy came off the field, Dawn and Carla ran to greet them. Dawn gave Nathan a big hug.

"You were great!" she exclaimed. "What a great pass to set up that last goal!"

He grinned. "Thanks. It was pure luck, though. If that guy hadn't missed the head shot, I wouldn't have had the ball."

Karin came walking across the field to join them. "You know how tough it is to scream, 'Yea Academy!' and then go 'Yea Nathan, Yea Troy' so that no one else can hear? I'm exhausted!"

Troy and Nathan headed for the showers, and the girls talked for a few minutes about the concert before Carla waved goodbye and headed home. When the boys reappeared, the foursome began walking the seven blocks to the pizza place.

"Mom's coming to get us around 8:30," Nathan said. "She didn't want us walking home, especially now that it's getting so dark."

"Colder, too," Karin said, shivering. "All of a sudden, it seems like fall is over."

"It is," Dawn said, taking Nathan's arm and leaning closer to him. "Next week we play our last two games, and then soccer's over."

"Wish we didn't have to play each other," Karin said as they reached the restaurant. "Then I wouldn't have to put up with Wendy."

"She's changed," Dawn said hopefully. "I don't think she's out for blood anymore."

"Good. Then she can just give me the scoring trophy, and we'll all go home, okay?" They all laughed and rounded the corner, nearly running head-on into two adults and a teenage girl. She looked at them with shock and surprise, first glaring at Karin and Troy and then at Dawn and Nathan.

"What is it?" the man asked, noting his daughter's expression.

"Nothing," she answered in a bitter tone. "Let's go!"

112

The parents exchanged a bewildered look before nodding to the foursome and trailing after her.

"Uh-oh," Dawn said softly.

"Tell me I just imagined seeing Wendy and her folks," Nathan said.

"Nope," Dawn said. "It really happened."

"Look, you can't let it worry you," Karin reassured Dawn as they finished their pizza.

"I know. But I'm sure she'll figure there's no way you and I can be friends and rivals at the same time—especially with the big game coming up next week, and the two of you fighting it out for the scoring lead," Dawn lamented. "She'll probably figure I'm going to do something to help you win that trophy."

"We may be friends, but that won't ever affect the way we play soccer against each other. If we go one-on-one, I'll do my best to score, even if it means ramming the ball right down your throat. And you'll be going just as hard to stop me. Can't Wendy understand that people can be friendly competitors?"

"No, she can't. You saw the way she looked at us. I'm sure she's home right now thinking terrible thoughts about both of us and how we've been plotting to keep her from getting her precious trophy."

"Don't let it get you down," Nathan interjected, laying a reassuring hand on Dawn's shoulder. "The kids who really count know that you two would never do anything like that."

She stared gloomily at the table, and Troy used the moment of silence to steer the conversation toward the next night's concert.

By the time Nathan's mother arrived, they were talking and laughing again, working on plans for Saturday. After dropping Troy and then Karin, they pulled up to Dawn's house. Nathan walked her to the door.

"Listen, I really don't want you to worry about Wendy," he said. "I meant what I said at the restaurant. Being friends with Karin is important. You've made her feel welcome at youth group, too, and what we're doing there is even more important." He smiled. "Cheer up, Dawn. I'm really glad we're friends."

Dawn smiled at him. "Me, too."

He squeezed her hand gently. "See you tomorrow night for the concert."

He hurried down to the car, and Dawn waved as a warm feeling rushed over her. Then she sighed again, but it was a determined sigh.

"You're just going to have to make her understand, God," she said aloud. "And, if she doesn't, then please help me show her how."

The concert was packed, and Dawn and Nathan squeezed into their seats by her parents just as the lights dimmed. They had greeted people at the door, explaining their needs and asking for support through free will donations. Nearly everyone had given something, and they had carefully gathered the money and handed it to Rev Steve.

At first they found it hard to concentrate on the music, but soon they were caught up in the exuberance of the first piece—a number in which, to Dawn's surprise and delight, Susan played a solo part on her violin.

She joined in a thunderous ovation as the number ended and the conductor singled out Susan for a bow. A thrill went through her as the slender, pretty young woman acknowledged the applause.

"She's great!" Nathan exclaimed.

"Not bad for an old lady soccer player," Dawn answered.

"Huh?"

"Oh, nothing," she chuckled. "Inside joke."

114

12
Injured

The kids sat on the edge of their chairs, fidgeting with anticipation. Rev Steve stood in front, holding out a bag. "Well," he said, "what do you think?"

"Five hundred?" someone asked.

"I'm going all out," Troy jumped in. "I'm guessing a thousand dollars, 'cause there sure was a lot of money in that sack, and everyone gave something."

"Well," Rev Steve began, "It wasn't five hundred and it wasn't a thousand, but—" he held up his free hand as several kids began to moan. "Would you all be happy with two thousand?"

"Dollars?" Monica sputtered, as a small gasp rippled through the group. There were a few seconds of stunned silence, and then they erupted into cheers.

"Did we really make two thousand dollars?" Karin asked.

"Not exactly," he answered. He held up a hand again as a couple of groans escaped from his charges. "Exactly, we made $2,086.27. Exactly." He grinned as the group cheered again. "Good job, everyone."

"With the car wash money, that puts us up to nearly $2,500," Nathan said. "Do you think we could get someone to haul the food to Chicago if we promised to pay them the rest in the next few weeks?"

"I think that there's more than a chance," Rev Steve replied. "I spoke to a trucking friend of mine this morning, and he said he'd take the load for whatever amount we had by the end of this week."

Again the room erupted in cheers, and the minister wiped at his eyes. "Kids," he said, his gentle voice filled with emotion, "I want you to know how proud of you I am. You tackled a big job, and you did it well. I've seen hunger and poverty in some of our big cities, and I know just how grateful these people are going to be to get this food."

They crowded around him, giving him hugs and thanks of their own for his confidence in them.

"If every group of kids was as determined as you are," he said, "it wouldn't take this old world very long to get back on the right track."

It was a warm October day, and Dawn bubbled with enthusiasm as she and her parents walked home from church. It wasn't until later that afternoon that she started thinking again about Wendy, and her bubble burst. The next day was going to be a problem, she thought, remembering again the hurt and angry look on Wendy's face at Friday evening's encounter.

"Problems?" her mother asked, looking up from the Sunday paper as Dawn came into the living room.

"Maybe. I think I'm in for some trouble with Wendy again."

"Oh, no," Mom exclaimed. "You just told us how you thought you might end up being friends."

Settling onto the couch, she told her parents about it. "I'm sure Wendy's got me down as a complete traitor for even talking with Karin."

"What do you think you should do?" Dad asked.

"*Nothing*. I like Karin; she's my friend. I *could* like

116

Wendy, too. I know we could be friends, if she'd just quit being so . . . oh, I don't know what she is, but her thing with Karin is stupid."

"You're absolutely right," her mother replied. "So why are you worried? Are you afraid of Wendy?"

Dawn was startled at the question.

"I—I don't think I'm afraid of her, but I'm worried about what she might say to the other girls. I don't want anyone thinking I'm not loyal to the team or anything, and I don't want them down on me. Does that make sense?"

"Absolutely." She smiled. "But, like I said, you're right. Stick to your beliefs and you'll be all right."

Dawn smiled. "Okay. Thanks for listening." She gave them each a hug and then headed for bed. Despite their reassurances, she knew it was going to be a tough day tomorrow.

It turned out to be even worse than she expected. The first confrontation came immediately, as the girls were changing into their practice gear.

"So, how's your friend from Academy?" Wendy sneered. "Have you got it all figured out how you can help them win?"

"Don't be stupid," Dawn snapped. "I'm not helping Academy win, and you know it. As for Karin—she's my friend, and I'm proud of it. And whether you like it or not, she's coming back to North Park next year. I've been working out with her almost every Saturday for the last five weeks, so I know she wants to be with us again as a teammate."

Wendy stared at her in disbelief. "What do you mean working out with her? You two have been practicing together?"

"Sure," Dawn replied. "What's wrong with that?"

"She's our enemy. We're supposed to be trying to beat them, and you're working with her. By now, she probably knows every special play we have."

"Oh, come off it, Wendy," Dawn said, pursing her lips in disgust. "Having her work against me has made me a better defender. Besides, she wants to come back here again next year, and I want her to. She'll be good for our team."

The rest of the girls were watching Dawn and Wendy with looks of shock and dismay. "So that's it," Wendy jumped up as she spoke. "You want to get her back here so she can be our top scorer, right? I suppose you've got it all figured out how to help her win that scoring trophy this year, too. You going to let her make a few extra shots against us on Saturday?"

Dawn reddened at the accusation. "That's crazy! And you're crazy for even thinking it!" she half shouted. Tears came into her eyes, and she wiped them away. She grabbed her shoes and ran outside.

Dawn was sitting by herself against the wall when Carla came out to join her. Several other girls glanced her direction and moved on toward the practice field without speaking.

"I suppose she's got everyone against me by now," Dawn remarked.

"No, but she's trying," Carla said. "Don't let it worry you. Some of them are wondering about you and Karin practicing together—but mostly they're figuring it's the same old Wendy spouting off. I told them how you and Karin have been friends all along, and it's no big deal. Come on. We've gotta get to practice." She held out a hand and helped Dawn to her feet.

Dawn wiped at her eyes again and tried a smile. "Thanks. I guess all my missionary work with Wendy is down the drain, huh? Well, at least part of this season was bearable. Sometimes she makes me so mad!" She took a deep breath. "I wouldn't cheat. I'll just have to show her on the field."

"Show her what?" Carla said.

"When I play Karin, I'm going to shut her out," Dawn answered. "That should show Wendy that you can be friends and competitors, too. Right?"

"Let's hustle, people," Alan barked as they finished stretching exercises. "Tomorrow's a big game. If we don't win then, it doesn't matter what we do Saturday against Academy."

The girls sprinted to their positions, and Dawn set up on the defensive side and began trapping the shots as they came at her from all angles. The drill moved quickly, and soon the coach blew his whistle and signaled for a tackling drill.

"Divide into pairs! I want each girl about two feet from the ball. When I blow my whistle, I want you both to advance on the ball at the same time. Defenders, you try to roll the ball over the attackers' feet and gain control of it. If you kick the ball instead of tackling it, you lose a point. If you tackle the ball properly, you get the point."

Carla lined up against Dawn, and Jeannie faced Wendy. Susan stepped between them at the next break.

"Change this around!" she ordered. "Dawn and Wendy; Carla and Jeannie!" Wendy moved grudgingly over to take Carla's place, glaring at Dawn as she did so.

"Let's go!" Susan signaled Alan, and he blew his whistle.

The girls sprinted to the ball and Wendy won the race, touching the ball neatly past Dawn and avoiding the tackle. Up-and-down the field, similar mini-battles were won or lost.

The coach blew his whistle to line them up again. "Ready?" he shouted.

Dawn eyed the ball, avoiding eye contact with Wendy. At the sound of the whistle, she raced to the ball, hooked her toe under it, and lifted it neatly over Wendy's foot as Wendy advanced.

Wendy turned and slashed at Dawn's heel with her own toe, nearly tripping Dawn in the process.

"Watch it!" Dawn warned.

"Watch it yourself!" Wendy responded. They exchanged angry looks, and Dawn bent down to pick up the ball. Seeing her advantage, Wendy reached over and gave Dawn a little shove. Dawn went sprawling and Wendy chortled, spinning quickly to retake her position as Dawn grasped the ball and sat up.

"You'll get suspended if you throw that thing," Wendy said arrogantly. As she passed Dawn, her toe snagged in the turf next to Dawn's foot and she stumbled, falling hard. She rolled over, a shocked expression on her face, then grabbed at her ankle—the one she'd been favoring earlier in the season—and yelled.

Susan came running and so did Alan, while Dawn scrambled on her hands and knees to Wendy's side.

"Why did you trip me?" Wendy gasped.

"What happened?" the coach demanded.

"She tripped and fell. It was an accident," Dawn said.

"She did it to me," Wendy sobbed, pointing at Dawn. "Get away from me, you traitor! You did that to me on purpose!" She continued sobbing as more of her teammates gathered around, and both coaches began checking her ankle.

Dawn stood, tears filling her own eyes. "It was an accident," she told Carla, as Carla gave her an uneasy glance. Several of the other girls looked from Wendy, now writhing in obvious pain, to Dawn, their eyes filled with accusations but their lips silent.

"It's true!" she exclaimed. "I didn't trip her; she just fell." She looked around at the others. "You don't believe me, but it's true. I didn't do anything to her! She slipped and fell." Tears streaming down her face, she turned and ran from the field, feeling the accusing stares of the others following her every step.

Her parents listened sympathetically as Dawn relayed the whole afternoon's happenings. Her eyes were still red from crying, but she had a determined sound to her voice.

"The other kids don't believe me—not even Carla. That's what hurts more than anything," she said bitterly. "But I didn't do anything. I'm just going to have to go back there and make them listen to me."

"That's the spirit," her dad said, coming over to sit beside her and putting a comforting arm around her shoulders. "If you tell them everything like you just told us, it'll be fine."

The telephone rang, and her mother jumped up to answer it, but Dawn held up a hand. "Wait, Mom, let me. It's probably one of the girls or the coaches calling."

"Hello?" she said, dabbing again at her eyes.

"Is this Dawn?" a rough male voice began. "This is Wendy Marks's father."

"Oh, hello, Mr. Marks," Dawn said softly. She glanced toward her parents.

"I've heard all about what happened today, and I just wanted to tell you personally that I think you should be ashamed of what you did and what you've been doing." His harsh voice stunned Dawn.

"I, uh—what do you mean?" she stammered.

"I mean that practicing with a member of one of your top opposing teams is about as unsportsmanlike as you can get. Like my daughter, I consider it traitorous to your own team!"

"But we weren't—" Dawn began.

"And another thing you should be happy to know,"

he said, cutting her off. "You won't have to worry about my daughter getting in your way any more this year, or about your friend from Academy winning the scoring trophy. You know why?" He hurried on, barely giving Dawn time for a breath. "Wendy's in the hospital to-night—and when she gets out tomorrow, she'll be on crutches and wearing a cast."

"What happened?" Dawn exclaimed.

"Thanks to you, young lady, my daughter tore the ligaments in her ankle today. She'll miss the rest of this soccer season!"

Before Dawn could react, he hung up the phone.

"We need to talk this out right now, or we might as well go onto the field and tell them we surrender." Alan spoke quietly to Dawn just outside the locker room door.

She wiped away tears and nodded. It had been the most miserable school day in her memory. Word had spread quickly about Monday's incident. Wendy's absence from school and word that she had ended up in a cast added fuel to the fire. Even Carla had been ten-tative in her support, although she offered Dawn a friendly word as they entered the gym.

"If you tell me you didn't trip Wendy, I believe you," Alan was saying now, as they walked to the locker room. "I think most of the girls do, too. The thing everyone's most concerned about is the practicing with Karin."

"I can explain that. It's really not like it sounds."

"Good." Alan smiled. "Let's go in there and get it cleared up, so we can get our team back together. Okay?"

Dawn nodded again and pushed open the door. "Coach is coming in," she said gruffly. "Everybody de-cent?"

No one spoke, so she turned back to Alan and said, "It's okay. Come on in."

122

"I'd like everyone to gather around here," Alan began, pointing to a couple benches. The girls complied, looking expectantly toward them as they found places to sit.

Dawn swallowed hard. "What I want to say first is that I did *not* trip Wendy or hurt her. We were arguing; that's true. But when she turned past me, she just slipped and fell. You can believe it or not, but it's the truth. She told me earlier that her ankle was bothering her, and I think she just injured it worse when she fell."

Dawn stopped and looked around. No one spoke. She took a deep breath and continued. "And I suppose you're wondering about me and Karin. Well, you see—"

"I put her up to that!" interrupted a voice.

Dawn swung around in surprise and found Rev Steve standing beside Susan in the doorway. He walked over to Dawn's side, draping his arm around her shoulders and giving her an encouraging smile.

Susan stepped to the front of the group. "Rev Steve heard about what was happening here and called me to explain. I thought he should tell all of you, too."

"As I just said, I was the cause of Dawn practicing with Karin," he repeated. "I want to tell you why I did it and why it wasn't wrong." He took his arm from Dawn's shoulders and moved into the midst of the girls. "When Dawn decided to come out for soccer this year, she asked me to help her with defense. It soon became obvious that we needed someone else to give us a little offense."

He straightened his shoulders and coughed before continuing. "Karin goes to my church; Dawn does, too. So do a couple others here. They work together and pray together and achieve together in our youth forum. They've done well." He glanced back at Dawn and gave her a big smile.

"The point I'm trying to make is that just because those girls went to different schools didn't mean that they couldn't work together on something they both believed in. In our youth group, that was a hunger project. Most of you have heard something about that, because I think everybody in the city got bugged into going to that concert last week."

The girls laughed nervously, and Rev Steve grinned.

"That's how it was with our soccer workouts, too. Dawn and Karin worked together to make something better—in this case, it was themselves as players. I'm sure you've all noticed that Dawn has turned into a pretty decent sweeperback, right?"

A murmuring of "yeses" and "greats" ran through the group.

"Some of that is due to me." He puffed himself up, and the girls broke into laughter this time.

"Some of it is due to Karin, because she provided the offensive shots to help Dawn improve. But most of it was due to Dawn herself. She put in the extra hours; she worked hard; and she became a winner." He backed up beside her and put his arm around her again. "If Dawn is guilty of anything, she's guilty of working hard to make your team a better team, because what she did on her own made you all winners.

"Of course, because of all her hard work, she's made Karin a darn good player, too. So, for that reason, maybe, you can be upset—especially since you still have to play against her." He paused as some of the girls started to giggle. "Now, you can be angry at her because you think she did something wrong—which she didn't. Or, you can be proud of her because she helped bring your team to the point where you have a shot at winning the conference championship this week.

"If I were you, I'd come up here and renew your friendship with a great girl, and then get out there as a

124

team and show Brownsville just how far you've come. With or without Wendy, you're a fine soccer team, and you can win both this game and Saturday's game because of it." He smiled, and then yelled, "Right?"

"Right!" they shouted in response, breaking into cheers. The girls surged forward, laughing and hugging Dawn as the minister accepted a handshake from Alan. Wiping away tears, Dawn walked over to Rev Steve's side.

"Thanks," she began, "I—I don't know . . ."

"You're welcome," he boomed, giving her another big hug. "Now, get out on that field and show 'em what you're made of. And Carla," he added, as she reached over to grasp Dawn's hand, "the offense is up to you and Tricia now, okay?"

"I'm going to get a goal, for sure—for Dawn," she answered.

"That's the spirit." He took Alan by the arm and headed him toward the door. "Come on, coach; let's get out of here so your star defender can get changed." He grinned at Dawn and gave her a thumbs-up. "After the victory, Dawn, you and I have one more visit to make before we go home."

"Wendy's?" she asked.

"Wendy's," he responded, giving her yet another thumbs-up and then ducking out the door.

13
Showdown

At halftime, Brownsville and North Park had struggled to a 0-0 tie. Twice the Polars had penetrated to the Orioles' goal area, only to be thwarted on great defensive plays—one by the center fullback and the other by the goalkeeper. As the girls came off the field, they each grabbed a cup of water and then sat down next to Alan.

"We've been this close twice," an exasperated Carla began, holding her thumb and forefinger about an inch apart. "I don't know what we can do any better to get the ball into the goal."

"I do," Susan replied, taking the portable chalkboard from Alan's hand and holding it up for everyone to see. "Each of the times we've been in scoring position, we've had at least three of our forwards on the attack, right?"

The girls nodded.

"But each time, one of you has pulled back at the last second, and we've botched the play. We've gotten too used to Wendy taking that final pass and then making a great move to score. Well, girls, we don't have Wendy. So you've got to do it on your own. And that means you've *all* got to stay on the attack right up until the shot is made."

She drew a diagram on the board, putting three forwards in a line just in front of the goal—one sweeping in from either side and one coming straight down the center. Then she drew Xs showing the center defender and the keeper.

"One of these times down, you're going to find yourself in this position again," she continued. "If one of the wings has the ball, I want you to get it to the center forward, but keep advancing toward the goal. Just be careful not to get offside." They nodded. "Then Carla or Tricia, if one of you is in that center spot, I want you to make a move on the defender and make her pick you up. As soon as she commits, get the ball off either right or left, and whoever takes the pass, shoot—right now!"

"Whatever you do, don't call for the ball," Alan inserted. "Just be looking for it—expect it. If you keep quiet, neither the fullback nor the keeper will know where the ball is going, and we'll be in position to score."

The referee blew his whistle to signal the second period, and the girls broke onto the field toward their areas. Nearly ten minutes passed before the opportunity arose. Dawn trapped a crossing pass as the Orioles moved onto the attack and, mustering all her strength, delivered the ball well past the middle of the field to Dotty Washington. Dotty controlled the ball, touched it over to Carla, and then cut behind her downfield. Tricia took the right wing, and suddenly they were in a three-on-one situation against the center fullback.

"Keep it, Carla, keep it!" Dawn muttered, moving forward in anticipation. Carla did just that, finally forcing the fullback to make a move. At that precise second, she passed to Tricia, who took the shot. The goalie grabbed at the ball, tipped it slightly, and watched in frustration as it found the near corner of the net.

That single goal stood up, and the happy Polars

romped around the field in a joyous victory lap after exchanging handshakes with the disappointed Brownsville squad. After the lap, they gathered around Dawn and the defenders to congratulate them on the shutout; then they carried Tricia from the field and tossed her into the shower.

Dawn took her time getting dressed, basking in the victory. When she quietly walked from the locker room, she found both her parents and Rev Steve waiting.

After hugging her mother, she turned toward the minister. "Thought you still might be waiting."

"You nervous?"

She nodded. "Yeah, but it's the right thing to do." She glanced at her parents. "You're not coming too, are you?"

"Do you want us to?" asked Dad.

She shook her head. "No, but I'm glad you waited for me here. I'll see you at supper."

The late October evening was cool and already dark, though it was barely past five-thirty. Dawn and Rev Steve said little as they walked to Wendy's house, and Dawn took a deep breath before ringing the bell.

Wendy's mother opened the door, spotted Dawn, and did a double take.

"May we come in?" the minister asked, not giving her time to speak.

She stepped back and ushered them in, then led them into the living room. Wendy was sitting in a large chair in front of the television, a pair of crutches lying beside her. Her foot, encased in a cast, was elevated on a stool. She glanced over her shoulder as they entered.

"What're you doing here?" she said, anger in her voice. She started to move forward in the chair, but the minister intervened.

"Sit back, Wendy. Dawn and I have something to talk with you about—and your mother, too," he quick-

128

ly added as Mrs. Marks moved toward the door. She walked slowly to her daughter's side and leaned against the back of the chair.

Motioning to Dawn to sit on the couch, Rev Steve began his explanation. When he was done, he held up his hands. "That's it."

"No, that's not it," Dawn said, standing up. "I want you to know that I didn't trip you on the field. I'm sorry you got hurt, Wendy, but you know I didn't do it. You just slipped and fell, and that's the honest-to-God truth." She stared at the other girl.

Wendy hung her head. "Yeah, I guess," she finally said.

"Wendy, what are you saying?" her mother said. "I thought you told us you were tripped."

"I—I'm not really sure," she shrugged. "Maybe I just slipped." She spoke softly, then grimaced and turned toward Dawn. "I guess I just wanted to blame you because of your friendship with Karin. I was mad." A tear trickled down her face and she paused to wipe it away. "Now, I won't even have a shot at that scoring title. That makes me angrier than anything. You know?"

Dawn walked over and laid a hand on Wendy's shoulder. "I guess I do know. You probably could have ended up scoring more points than Karin in these last games—especially in the final game Saturday."

"And especially with Dawn on your team," Rev Steve added.

"Huh?" the girls said simultaneously.

"What do you mean?" Wendy asked.

"I mean that Dawn's turned into the best defensive player in the league. I'll be amazed if Karin gets more than one goal on Saturday, but you would probably score a couple for the Polars."

He paced across the room and continued.

"I've been watching this team all year, Wendy, and

129

everyone knows that you're the star when it comes to scoring. But you've been so concerned with your own statistics that you haven't stopped to think that it's a *team* you're playing with. North Park's success this year hasn't been just because you scored a lot of points, but because your teammates got you the ball, and Dawn and the other defenders kept the other teams off the scoreboard."

Wendy hung her head and looked away, a hurt expression on her face.

"Why don't you come out to the big game this Saturday," he concluded, "and admire the fine team you've been playing with all year. They defeated Brownsville today, and they did it as a team. You really should watch them play."

Wendy didn't return to school the rest of the week. Dawn wavered between calling her and visiting her again, but finally did neither. She also chose not to tell her teammates about the Tuesday night encounter at Wendy's house. But on Friday night, after a final, jittery practice session, she went home and phoned Karin.

"Well, tomorrow is *it*," Dawn emphasized, leaning back against the wall as she talked. "I don't know about you, but I'm glad the season is about over. I really wish we didn't have to go against each other."

"Me, too," Karin replied. "This'll be the last time, though. I'm definitely coming back to North Park next year. I don't know about soccer yet, but I guess that's not the most important thing, anyway."

Dawn smiled into the phone. "That's the way I've been feeling, too. The main thing is that we're together as friends.

"How many goals did you get Tuesday?" She continued, changing the subject.

"Zilch. Got shut out," Karen replied.

130

"You're kidding."

"No, really. I only played half the game, and it seemed like every time I was in position to shoot, one of the other girls had a better position, so I just passed a lot. Coach wanted us to take it easy on Edgemont, since they haven't won a game all year. He hardly played the starters—saving us for you guys, I guess."

"Good thing," Dawn said. " 'Cause we're going to give you a real battle." She laughed. "Anyway, good luck tomorrow, but not too much."

"Yeah, thanks. We're not on the same side yet, you know, so you better be sharp or I'm going to leave you lying in the dust."

"Hah!" Dawn exclaimed. "Fat chance!"

They giggled again and then went silent, thinking about the confrontation.

Karin finally broke the silence. "Take care."

"Okay. See you on the field."

For the second time that week, Dawn spent a restless night, tossing and turning and waking up almost on the hour. Her dreams were of dozens of soccer balls coming at her, all at the same time—and Wendy standing accusingly beside her, leaning on her crutches and pointing out her defensive mistakes on each shot.

Feeling depressed, she finally got up around eight o'clock. The weather had changed overnight, and it was a cool, cloudy day. Dawn made her way down to the breakfast table feeling cranky and on edge, but her parents had left for an auction sale, and she had no one to complain to. She ate a bowl of cold cereal and then settled in front of the television to watch a cartoon.

At eleven-thirty her parents still hadn't returned, so she wrote them a note, had a ham and cheese sandwich with a glass of milk, and started for the school. About halfway there, she met Carla. They walked on together, reaching the gym just as the first rain started to fall.

By game time, it was raining steadily. The girls knew it was going to be a long, hard afternoon. As they walked from the gym to the field, Nathan came over to greet Dawn.

"Came to wish you luck," he smiled, holding out both hands. She clasped his hands and nodded, then jogged nervously onto the field.

Academy's Chieftans were already warming up, and Karin hurried over to say hello. The field was turning muddy.

"Hey, what's happening over by your bench?" Karin inquired as they stood together at center field.

Dawn looked around. "It's Wendy," she exclaimed. "Look, I better go over there, too. Good luck." She made her way to the bench where everyone was talking with Wendy. As Dawn approached, a couple of the other girls stepped out of the way.

"Hi," Wendy greeted her, her face lighting up.

"Hi yourself," Dawn answered. "How's the ankle?"

"It'll be okay." She smiled and turned to Alan. "Can I say something to the team before they go back out?"

"Of course," Alan replied. He signaled for everyone to sit down.

"So, you guys, this is it, you know?" Wendy began. The other girls laughed nervously at her opening. "I want you to know that I think you should win today, and that I'm sorry I can't be out there playing with you. Not that I think you need me to win." She swallowed hard and looked around. "You don't. You're a good, strong team.

"Most of the year, I've been a real jerk. And the way I acted with Dawn the other day was the jerkiest thing of all." She leaned forward on her crutches and extended a hand to Dawn. "I want you all to know that Dawn didn't do anything to hurt me, and I'm proud to have her as a teammate and, uh . . . ," she paused, ". . . as a friend."

Dawn stepped forward and gave Wendy a hug, and the other girls cheered.

Wendy clapped her hands together in front of her crutches and then held out a hand to slap the palm of each teammate as the girls ran by to retake the field.

Dawn stopped as Wendy's father approached, carrying the scoring trophy wrapped in a large piece of plastic. Water was dripping off the plastic and off their faces, too, as the rain intensified. Dawn looked uneasily at the man who had yelled at her on the phone and then pointed to the trophy.

"It's beautiful."

"Yes," he said. "I wanted Wendy to win it, but maybe that's why she ended up getting hurt. I heard how she'd been hiding that sore ankle from everyone. I guess I put too much pressure on her." He smiled and put his arm around his daughter. "I want to apologize for the way I acted with you, too. You're a fine young woman, and you didn't deserve to be treated as I treated you."

Dawn blushed slightly.

"Anyway," he continued. "As much as it pains me, I'm going to hang around and give this to an Academy girl after the game."

"Maybe not," Dawn said quickly. "She has to score first, you know."

"What do you mean?" Wendy asked.

"Karin didn't score on Tuesday, so you're still tied. If she gets a goal on us today, she's really going to have to earn it! You think maybe you could get a second one of those trophies, Mr. Marks? You may have co-winners." She grinned, slapped hands with Wendy, and raced onto the field as the teams began setting up.

It soon became apparent that it was going to be a battle between the elements and the girls as much as between the two teams. Time and again players from both sides slipped, fell, or slid out of plays in the wet and muddy field.

By halftime, it was still a 0-0 tie. A few snow flurries mixed with the rain caused the coaches to huddle with the officials before deciding to continue.

"We've got to go on," Alan said, hustling over to the sidelines after the meeting. "Our only alternative is to call it a tie, and then Academy will take the title by a game. I told them we'd rather lose in the snow than lose by default."

The girls cheered, and he brightened. "Glad to hear you agree with me."

Wendy hobbled over to where they were huddling around the coach and shouted to get his attention. He joined her for a few seconds, then called the others over. "Wendy's got a suggestion," he said, "and I like the sound of it." He nodded to her. "Go ahead."

"The middle of the field is where you're always slipping and falling," said Wendy. "But I've seen Dotty make some good crossing passes off that far touchline corner. Why not try to get the ball to her down there and then get the other forwards together just outside the penalty area. If Dotty can get the ball up, you all have to go up for the head shot and just try to punch it in." She shrugged. "What've you got to lose?"

They looked at each other and nodded agreeably.

"Okay," Alan broke in. "Let's try it. Next time down, hit the touchline right away and stay on Dotty; then find the firmest ground you can and make your pass. Come on, Polars. This is it! Give me all you've got. You can rest up all winter!" He and Susan stood together and held out their hands. The girls crowded around, tightly clasping their hands together.

"Coach," Dawn interrupted. "I asked this the first game; I want to ask it again. A quick prayer?"

Alan looked around, and several girls nodded. He did the same.

"Lord," Dawn said, "keep us all safe now and give us the strength to play the best that we can. Amen."

"Amen," several others echoed. Then, "Let's go get 'em, Polars!"

"For Wendy!" Dawn added.

"Yeah! For Wendy!" they yelled together. They broke the huddle and raced onto the field. Dawn glanced Wendy's direction and gave her the high sign before hurrying to her area as the whistle blew.

It took more than ten minutes, but finally the opportunity came. Tricia took a lead pass from Trini after Trini had cut off Academy's pass attempt. Tricia dribbled once and blasted a pass to the right touchline where Dotty had seen her chance. The Polar forward ran Wendy's suggestion to perfection, dribbling deep to the corner and drawing the left fullback with her. Tricia, Amy Zobel—filling Wendy's spot—and Carla converged on the penalty area, and Dotty eluded the fullback and lofted her crossing pass.

The ball sailed in high, just missing the center fullback and Carla, but falling neatly between Tricia and Amy. For a split second they hesitated, not sure who should take the ball; then Tricia threw herself toward it and headed the shot hard and fast past the outstretched hands of the goalie for the score.

"Now we've just gotta hold 'em. Play tough!" Dawn said firmly.

The next five minutes tested their resolve to the limit.

Twice Karin attacked, once stripping the ball from Tricia and penetrating just outside the danger zone and once cutting off a Polar pass and breaking into the zone just behind Trini to take a hard, low shot. Both times the defense held, and Beth made a great stop and punted the ball way back upfield. With three minutes

135

remaining, Karin had the ball again. She moved to the left corner touchline, as if taking a page from the Polar game plan.

At the last second, though, she touched the ball back between the diamond zone and tried a looping pass over Dawn to the Academy left winger. Dawn backpeddled to cut off the pass. Leaping high, she trapped the ball just below her chin, came down as the ball did, and tried a quick return kick.

Her left foot went sliding on the wet grass, and as she slipped her kick came back sideways instead of heading upfield. It went right back to Karin at three-quarter speed. Karin controlled the ball with her inside right thigh, then powered the shot into the near corner of the net. With just over two minutes remaining, the teams were tied at one.

"I blew it," Dawn whispered to herself, scuffing at the muddy field as Carla and Amy combined to kick off. Before she had time to chastise herself further, she was back on defense. Carla's pass was bad, and Karin charged through to control the ball again. She swiftly dibbled past Trini and challenged Dawn one-on-one. Dawn shifted, waving with her left hand for Beth to cover that side.

Karin bore down on her, as Trini scrambled to regain position and help out. Karin feinted to her right, but Dawn maintained eye contact and saw Karin's quick glance left. That's when Karin stopped and fired the shot. Dawn made her move to the side, trapped the shot, and rapidly delivered it upfield to Dotty.

Her response was so rapid that the Academy forwards and halfbacks were caught moving toward the Polar goal. But Carla was going the other way in pace with Dawn's kick, and Dotty took just one step with the ball before delivering a pass to the Polar forward.

Carla barely broke stride as she controlled the pass

with her left foot and hit the space between the sweeper and the left forward. Her momentum put her one-on-one with the goalie and a look of shock and fear swept across both girls' features. Carla took the shot—and scored.

As time expired, the Polars converged on Carla and buried her in a joyous heap. North Park had a 2-1 win and a share of the conference crown. It was only during the handshaking session with Academy that Dawn remembered: Karin's goal had won her the scoring title. A league official and photographer came walking onto the field, carrying the trophy, which was presented to Karin amid cheers from her Academy teammates and polite applause from the Polars.

As she congratulated Karin, Dawn looked around to the bench area where Wendy and her father had been standing. They were nowhere to be seen.

14
Drums & Bugles

After long, hot showers, Dawn and Carla emerged from the locker room to find that the rain had stopped, and the sun was hinting at breaking through the late afternoon clouds. Exhausted, they dragged themselves silently toward Dawn's house.

"Whose car is that?" Carla asked, as they approached the drive.

"Beats me." Dawn shrugged. She peered ahead as a man stepped from the car. "It's Wendy's dad! What's he doing here?"

He gave them a welcoming wave, walked around the passenger side, and pulled open the door. A pair of crutches emerged, followed by Wendy. "Hi." She greeted them with a smile. " 'Bout time. Seems like we've been waiting here for hours."

"S-Sorry," Dawn stammered. "I didn't know. . . ."

"Just teasing," Wendy interrupted. She grinned, then sobered. "Look. Dad and I have been waiting here to tell you again that we're both sorry about what happened earlier. You played a super game today." She grinned at Carla. "Both of you."

"I'm really sorry about the goal for Karin," Dawn

138

spoke rapidly. "I thought I had the kick away, and then. . . .

"Then you slipped," Wendy finished. "There was no way you could've done it any better. Now quit feeling sorry for yourself and accept a compliment, for pete's sake!"

They looked around at the sound of a horn, and a second car pulled in. It was Rev Steve, and riding beside him was Karin. Dawn sucked in sharply, and Wendy leaned back on her crutches. Karin stepped from the car with the scoring trophy in hand. She strode forward, a purposeful expression on her face.

Rev Steve trailed behind, the faint flicker of a smile on his face. "I was driving this way and found this wayward soccer player walking along," he said. "Seems like we were both going to the same place."

"Congratulations on the trophy," Wendy said before anyone else could speak. "You deserved it." She extended her hand as Karin stared at her in amazement.

Finally she reached over and grasped Wendy's hand. "Thanks." She finally spoke. "But I'm not keeping it."

"What?" The question came in unison from all the others.

"I'm giving it away—to Dawn."

Now it was Dawn's turn to stare at Karin in amazement. "But . . . why? I don't understand."

"It's simple," Karin said. "I've been doing some calculating, and I figure that you probably saved twice as many shots as both Wendy and I made all year. That makes you the real scoring champion in my book, and that's why I'm giving you the trophy." She extended the beautiful trophy with both hands, but Dawn just shook her head.

"No, I can't. Really."

Rev Steve moved forward and grasped the trophy. "Since no one really seems to want this little baby, I

139

have a suggestion. Let's build a little case and put it up in North Park High School—in a place where each of you can see it in the years ahead and remember that it almost interfered with some even bigger trophies— friendship and respect." He gazed at it for a few seconds. "What do you say?"

"Perfect!" Dawn exclaimed with a jubilant smile.

"I agree," Wendy said. "That is, if Karin's really going to join us at North Park next year." She gave Karin an inquisitive glance. "Are you?"

"Yes," Karin answerd. "But I don't know about soccer. I think friendships at school are more important—"

"Hey, wait a minute!" Wendy cut her off. "You better play soccer next year. We've already got the best defender in the state. Now with Carla and Tricia playing so great, we could have the best bunch of forwards in the state, if . . ." she paused. "If you join us, too. And I mean that." She extended her right hand, palm up, and gave Karin a questioning glance.

Karin hesitated a few seconds before grinning broadly and slapping Wendy's palm with her own right hand.

"All right," Carla said exuberantly. "We'll all win a trophy. The state championship trophy!"

"Well, now that everyone's patting everyone else on the back, I still think Dawn deserves a little trophy of her very own," Rev Steve cut in. "So, I have a presentation to make." He stopped and reached inside his coat pocket, pulling out a small trophy stand. On top was mounted a tiny drum and tiny gold bugle.

Karin was the first to speak. "What's that?"

"Ta-ta-ta-ta, brrrrum," Rev Steve answered. "That's a bugle and a drum roll—a little something that only hard-working defenders can understand."

"Yeah," Dawn said, clutching the tiny trophy close as her friends applauded. "And it's the best drums and bugles I've ever heard."

ANDREA'S BEST SHOT

This new girl could mean trouble!

Andrea's last year at Brown Junior High might be a good one after all. With their new coach, who also teaches Andrea's Sunday school class, the girls' basketball team is off to a great start. So is Andrea's relationship with Matt.

But Andrea is worried about the way her friend Jill has been acting since she started to hang around the new girl from the air force base. It could ruin their friendship—and wreck the whole team's chance to enter their first tournament ever.

The team will need more than a good hook shot to pull off a victory . . .

DAN JORGENSEN, active in sports and journalism, lives in Minnesota with his wife and two daughters.